Lucas couldn't miss the flash of excitement in her eyes, or the way her fingers pressed into his forearm.

All those signs of her hunger fueled his. Reminded him that he wasn't in this haze of desire alone.

Lucas dropped his forehead to hers, his heart slamming against his ribs. "In the interest of making sure we're on the same page, what do you want to happen?"

He needed to be clear. Needed her to be sure after the walls she'd carefully erected around herself.

But when Blair closed the distance between them, leaning into him with her delectable body, he realized he needn't have worried about that.

"I want you to make me forget everything but you, Lucas." Her hips rolled against his. "Please."

Hell.

Of all the ways she enticed him, it was the *please* that turned the last of his restraint to ashes.

* * *

Ways to Tempt the Boss by Joanne Rock is part of the Brooklyn Nights series.

Dear Reader,

Welcome back to the Brooklyn brownstone where three friends are working hard to turn their dreams into reality! This month, Blair Westcott is bringing her talents to the makeup industry, one face at a time. I love Blair because she sees the potential for beauty all around her, using her skills to enhance what's already there. Rather than craft a perfect face, she helps her clients *feel* beautiful.

Of course, Lucas Deschamps doesn't discover that right away. He sees a rebel adversary cloaked in pink and frills, someone who must be hiding an agenda behind the perpetual sunny smile. Because no one could be as sweet as Blair seems on the outside, could they? I think he'll feel bad once he realizes the dark secrets Blair hides are much different than he first believes.

Blair won't let anyone dim her sparkle, though, and I hope you won't, either.

Happy reading!

Joanne Rock

JOANNE ROCK

WAYS TO TEMPT THE BOSS

HARLEQUIN®
DESIRE™

Recycling programs
for this product may
not exist in your area.

ISBN-13: 978-1-335-73514-0

Ways to Tempt the Boss

Copyright © 2021 by Joanne Rock

Harlequin Enterprises ULC
22 Adelaide St. West, 40th Floor
Toronto, Ontario M5H 4E3, Canada
www.Harlequin.com

Printed in U.S.A.

Joanne Rock credits her decision to write romance after a book she picked up during a flight delay engrossed her so thoroughly that she didn't mind at all when her flight was delayed two more times. Giving her readers the chance to escape into another world has motivated her to write over eighty books for a variety of Harlequin series.

Books by Joanne Rock

Harlequin Desire

Brooklyn Nights

A Nine-Month Temptation
Ways to Tempt the Boss

Dynasties: Mesa Falls

The Rebel
The Rival
Rule Breaker
Heartbreaker
The Rancher
The Heir

Visit her Author Profile page at Harlequin.com, or joannerock.com, for more titles.

You can also find Joanne Rock on Facebook, along with other Harlequin Desire authors, at Facebook.com/HarlequinDesireAuthors!

To the caregivers, for your selflessness.

One

As corporate spies went, makeup artist Blair Westcott sure didn't seem the type.

Lucas Deschamps studied the newest hire for Deschamps Cosmetics from the shadows of a lighted set while his creative team prepared for a photo shoot in the West Village. Blair wielded an eyeliner brush with a steady hand as she created a cat's-eye on the model seated in her chair. Latin pop music poured from a Bluetooth speaker on the mirrored vanity table, a makeup kit unfolding like Russian nesting dolls on a cart nearby. A shoulder-length blond ponytail swung over one shoulder as she leaned forward to work on the Brazilian Olympic athlete who'd agreed to endorse the Deschamps brand.

Yet it wasn't the celebrated international volleyball player who captured his attention. That distinc-
tion went solely to Blair, whose black apron cinched
her waist and flared over hourglass hips. She laughed
and chatted as she worked, her warm manner putting
the other woman at ease, the same way it did with
everyone she encountered.

Except, of course, for Lucas. *Ease* was never what
he experienced around the talented makeup artist his
mother—founder of the brand—had hired without
consulting him. Not that Cybil Deschamps needed
his approval, since it was still technically her company. But with Lucas's estranged father attempting
to acquire the smaller brand as a way to undermine
his ex-wife, Lucas wished his mom had come to him
sooner to help stabilize the business. Lucas would
have recommended a hiring freeze in case his shady
father attempted to place a plant inside the company
to gather corporate intelligence. He wouldn't put it
past the guy.

Could Blair be that plant? It set off warning bells
in Lucas's head that her previous job was at a Long
Island-based beauty company owned by the luxury-
brand conglomerate headed by Lucas's father. Biting
back his frustration, Lucas sidestepped a photographer's assistant as the young woman dragged a floor
light off the set to make room for a fan. Another assistant passed Lucas a cup of black coffee he hadn't
asked for, but he accepted the mug while he added

up what he knew about the makeup artist currently sifting through a tray of eye-shadow palettes.

For starters, Blair Westcott seemed entirely too sweet. Too kind and warmhearted to be for real. She baked treats for the staff at Deschamps Cosmetics, for crying out loud. At least once a week since she started with the company six weeks ago, she showed up with plastic containers stuffed full of homemade cookies or cupcakes. Who did that? He tried to picture her juggling those big containers on the subway during rush hour and failed. Then again, she was also the sort of person others hastened to help. If Blair had been a cartoon princess, she would be the one that all of the forest animals followed around while they sang songs and cleaned her house. It was the Blair Effect.

And the quality was so noticeable, so unusual, that it made him wonder what she was hiding under the sunny exterior. He'd suspected there was a mole in the company dating back almost six weeks—the same time frame Blair had been hired. So he'd taken a closer look at her. In his experience, no one was as thoughtful and sweet as she appeared to be without an ulterior motive.

She raised red flags for him. Unfortunately, that wasn't the only thing she raised. Along with his suspicion of her, Lucas also felt hot, unrelenting attraction. The unwanted hunger ticked him off and made him perpetually surly around her, which hadn't exactly helped him figure her out.

"Would you like to take an advance peek, Lucas?"

The dulcet tone of Blair's voice yanked him from his dark thoughts, and he glanced up to meet the pale, blue-green eyes of his tormentor. She gestured toward the athlete she'd been working on for the photo shoot, then took a step back from her makeup chair, as if to leave him an unobstructed view of her work. Too bad it was all but impossible to tear his gaze from *her*. Her lips were so full they had a perpetual pouting quality. Her cheeks were just rounded enough to make the appearance of her dimples a surprise when she smiled. But it was her tall, curvy form that was the source of too many personal fantasies. There was an unapologetic femininity in the way she dressed that flattered every delectable inch of her. Today's frothy pink skirt and prim white blouse were typical of her wardrobe and shouldn't be so damn enticing.

She raised her eyebrows, clueing him in to the fact he'd been staring.

He felt himself scowl before he could restrain the reaction.

She only smiled wider and continued, "You were frowning so hard, I thought I'd better check in with you in case I'm using the wrong shades on Antonia?"

There, underneath the charming ways, he saw a flash of challenge in Blair's eyes. Maybe even a hint of "go screw yourself." He didn't think she showed that attitude to anyone but him, and it wasn't the first time he'd glimpsed the look that came and went in an instant. Everyone else saw her sweet side. He would swear there was plenty of fire beneath.

"The makeup is perfect," Lucas assured the young Olympian in the chair, figuring it would be safer to focus on her. "We really appreciate you working with us on the campaign."

He lifted his coffee mug in a toast, glad to deflect attention from the tension between him and Blair.

"My pleasure." Antonia gave him a nod of acknowledgement before leaning forward to scrutinize herself in the lighted mirror. "I'm grateful to Blair for making me look like myself instead of caking layers of foundation over all my freckles the way some makeup artists feel compelled to."

"The freckles are gorgeous." Blair peered into the glass over the other woman's shoulder, although it was his gaze she met in the reflective surface. "We wouldn't dream of covering them up," she practically cooed.

Or maybe it just sounded that way to his ears since, during a planning meeting for the shoot the week before, he'd suggested the close-ups of the mascara might be more dramatic with a more air-brushed quality to the skin around the eye. He hadn't considered it an indictment of freckles so much as a creative decision to showcase a product, but the art director and Blair had both taken the opposing view.

And Blair was enjoying the vindication, apparently.

"Are we almost ready?" he asked too sharply before gulping the black coffee too fast and scalding everything on the way down. "We want to keep Antonia on schedule."

His voice rasped from the burn as he set down the mug and shoved the drink away from him.

Blair's dimples appeared even as she bit her plump lower lip, and he was willing to bet she was struggling not to laugh.

"Of course." Blair whipped off the black protective drapery that had been covering Antonia. "I'll just let Jermaine touch up her hair on set."

Nodding, Lucas stalked back to the shadows of the photographer's studio, more than ready to view the results of the day on a laptop feed. Keeping his focus on the device was safer than watching Blair. Until he figured out her angle, he couldn't afford to trust her. And he definitely couldn't afford to indulge the attraction that gnawed at him more with each passing day.

Even if he was damn curious to know if she felt sparks on her end, too.

He only had a month left to help his mother make significant strides with Deschamps Cosmetics so they could secure the support of her board members in staving off a takeover by his father's conglomerate. The sooner he could settle this, the better. Lucas had his own business to run, a start-up that connected a highly skilled home-based workforce with companies that needed to outsource. He'd put his own professional life on hold in order to do this one favor for his mother. One last kindness to finally atone for not telling her that his father was a liar and a cheat back when he'd first discovered the truth about his dad.

If not for Lucas's silence as a teen, his mom would have started her cosmetics company under her own steam, with her maiden name attached, and she wouldn't be warding off BS corporate attacks like the one she faced now.

One more month and he'd be free of the debt he owed her. He just hoped he'd be free of the hold Blair Westcott had on him.

But to be sure of that, he withdrew his phone and emailed her a private message. Based on the way she'd baited him in front of the talent today, Lucas suspected the time had come to confront this heated awareness head-on.

And if he could tease out her possible corporate spying connections, so much the better.

See me in my office at 5pm.

Blair Westcott read and reread the ominous email subject line glaring at her from the top of her inbox once she got back to midtown headquarters that afternoon. There was no text in the body of the email. Not even an auto-filled signature that normally signaled the close of any Deschamps Cosmetics company message.

Not that Blair needed a signature to know who wanted to see her in his office at the end of the business day. Lucas Deschamps, heir apparent to his mother's cosmetics firm, had taken a personal dislike to her from their first meeting.

Damn it.

She couldn't think about Lucas and his suspicious tawny eyes right now. After closing the laptop at her desk on the floor full of junior employees at Deschamps Cosmetics, Blair paused near the snack station in the center of the desks and withdrew a thin throw blanket from a freshly laundered stack in a wicker basket at the end of one countertop. The open-concept offices on this floor maintained a temperature that was always on the cool side, and the company prided itself on preserving a relaxed work community for the creative team. So even during business hours, Blair could wrap herself in a throw and sit in one of the casual lounge chairs lining the wall of windows overlooking the Hudson River. From the perch forty-two stories high, she could watch cruise ships and barges sail past the Statue of Liberty while a few of her colleagues brainstormed lipstick names and played a game of table tennis.

Her phone buzzed with a notification just as she wiggled her way into a comfortable position in the lounge chair.

Are you coming up this weekend?

The text from her mother gave her conscience a jab as she thought about her sick mom alone in the little cabin Blair had rented for her an hour north of here, to be close to a good cancer center. Blair had quit her degree program and sold her mother's house in Long Island to finance the surgery her mom had needed when Amber Westcott had been diagnosed with ovarian cancer. Thanks to having no healthcare insurance when a visit to a walk-in clinic led to the diagnosis, the bills were through the roof, even when medical providers worked with them to find financial assistance for treatment. The cancer center Amber now attended for her therapy was well-rated, with the benefit of being in an area with a lower cost of living. On the weekends, Blair took a train that followed the Hudson River, then got off at a stop where she had to take an Uber to reach the picturesque spot in the foothills of the Catskill Mountains.

But the cost of the rented cabin and car fares were nothing compared to the price tag on the chemotherapy.

Definitely! Blair typed back quickly, adding a

string of emojis to sound cheery. I miss you! Feeling okay?

Tired, actually. You should stay home this weekend, sweetheart. I'm just going to sleep, anyway.

The knot in her belly tightened.

All the more reason I should come take care of you. Her fingers shook a little as she typed this time—Blair hated that she couldn't be with her mom 24/7 to look after her. Her father had remarried immediately following the divorce from Amber ten years ago, so he wasn't in the picture. And Blair was an only child. Which meant her mom really needed her now, even though one of her friends lived nearby and took her to her chemo appointments. Sat with her afterward. It wasn't the same as having family around. I'll make that chicken soup you like.

The next text took longer to arrive. She gripped the phone harder, as if that would make the answer come sooner.

Text me Friday, and I'll let you know how I feel. Napping now.

Blair sent a few kiss emojis.

Tugging the lightweight fleece blanket tighter around her, she closed her eyes against the pain that came with the concern for her mom's health. She'd parked herself in front of the view to distract herself from worries about her enigmatic, taciturn boss. Yet thinking about the way Lucas fixed his smoldering gaze on her would be better than the gut-wrenching fear she felt for her mom and how to pay for the health care necessary to keep her alive.

Because Blair couldn't accept the unusual job offer she had received three days ago from her previous employer. Not when the job involved gathering strategic competitive intelligence on Deschamps Cosmetics. It was completely unethical, even if she wouldn't have been doing anything technically illegal. She wouldn't have even listened to the pitch except that taking the job meant she would have been able to pay for the chemo treatments. The former colleague who'd contacted her with the proposition had gotten her hopes up at first, saying he had a moonlighting gig that would be the financial answer to her prayers. But when the assignment became clearer, Blair knew she couldn't be a spy. She'd have to find another way to afford the infusion therapy.

Especially since she'd only been able to take the job at Deschamps thanks to an affordable-housing option extended to her by Cybil Deschamps. More than just the founder of Deschamps Cosmetics, Cybil was also a prominent philanthropist and socialite who had donated one of her properties in Brooklyn as a trial "club residence for women," inspired by the historic Barbizon Hotel. Blair's shared apartment and the roommates who came with it were the brightest part of the most nerve-racking time of her life. So Cybil was the last person Blair would ever want to spy on, no matter how big the paycheck.

Her ex-coworker had insisted Blair continue to think it over for the week, however, making her feel guilty about the offer even though she hadn't accepted. The conversation was made even stranger by the woman's reminder that their communication was private and still covered under Blair's nondisclosure agreement from her former employer. That didn't seem possible now that she no longer worked for About Face, but she didn't argue the point since she didn't plan to discuss it, anyway.

"Hey, Blair," one of her male colleagues called to her over the noise of the table tennis game. "Tomorrow's Wednesday. That's cookie day, right?"

Rising from the beanbag chair, she turned to see multiple heads swing her way, her coworkers clearly interested in baked goods. She pasted on a smile to hide the inner turmoil over her mom and her constant worry about how to pay the medical bills. Besides, baking was her outlet. She liked bringing a little joy into the workplace every week. It was so much easier to do here than in her mom's lonely cabin.

"Cookies or cupcakes. I'm happy to make either." She peered around at the group gathered near a stand-up conference table—all of them seemed as invested in this discussion as the guys at the Ping-

Pong table. Then again, it was almost five o'clock, so the workday was winding down. "Any special requests?"

About twelve answers overlapped one another, a motley chorus of cookie names and cupcake flavors pelting her from every side.

Laughing, she shrugged off the blanket she'd been wearing like a cape, folding the ends together even though it would only end up in the washing machine tonight. She laid it neatly over the back of the chair at her desk.

"How about I choose?" she suggested, knowing her roommates would be glad for the sweets, too. Both Tana and Sable had hectic jobs, and Blair liked the way food brought them all together in the evenings. She needed their companionship to keep her sanity. "I'll bring two things, though. Cupcakes *and* cookies."

Cheers and a few wolf whistles greeted the news. She would have ended the day on this happy note if she hadn't been tasked to meet Lucas now.

Crap.

Retrieving a small handbag from under her desk, she resisted the urge to run a comb through her hair. She did grab a mint from her purse, though, telling herself she would do the same for a meeting with a woman. Fresh breath was always important in a one-on-one meeting. Not just the ones with ridiculously attractive bosses.

She bypassed the elevators to take the stairs since she only needed to go up one flight to reach the executive offices. Entering the stairwell, the heavy steel door echoed behind her as it shut. While she climbed the steps, she tried to psych herself up for the meeting. Lucas was on the board of directors at Deschamps Cosmetics, and Cybil had commented more than once that he would take her place as CEO within the year. But until recently, Lucas hadn't worked on site. He had his own firm, completely unrelated to makeup or the beauty industry, which made Blair wonder if he would really take over his mother's company one day or if that was just wishful thinking on his mom's part.

Either way, Blair was extremely wary of the tall, dark-haired business mogul who seemed to stare straight through her with his tawny-colored eyes. He didn't make her uneasy, exactly. More like…unsettled. His gruff manner of speaking didn't help matters, either. Far from putting her off, his brooding scowls only made her want to sidle closer. Tease a laugh from him.

Or a kiss.

Had she just thought that? Belatedly, she slammed that idea into a vault in her brain and locked it away where she couldn't revisit it. Ever.

She had no business thinking about her too-sexy boss that way. Even though right now, shoving through the heavy steel door that led onto the floor of the executive offices, Blair couldn't deny a surge of heat at the thought of being alone with him in his office.

Luckily, she'd gotten used to ignoring her feminine instincts where Lucas was concerned, since they'd fallen into a habit of baiting each other rather than confronting the way the temperature soared when they got within ten yards of one another.

Now, her high heels sinking in the plush carpet in the vacated reception area outside of Lucas's office, Blair popped a second mint. This one for nerves.

Because the only thing that mattered when it came to Lucas was doing her job. She couldn't afford to lose this paycheck while she continued her search for supplementary income.

Blowing out a breath, her fist was poised to knock when the door was yanked open so fast that it made the pane of glass in the sidelight rattle softly.

"Come in, for crying out loud." He stood framed in the doorway, glaring at her with the usual amount of heat.

She felt the smile unfurl, and realized she actually meant this one. It wasn't the socially acceptable polite mask of friendliness she wore with her coworkers. Or the cheerful face she wore around her mom and the medical staff to keep everyone upbeat. Something about Lucas's unorthodox behavior gave her license to not try so damn hard. And, call her crazy, that was a relief.

"Thank you, Lucas." She called him by his first name because he'd demanded as much at their first meeting. She found it hard to envision what he sounded like when he wasn't making demands. "I think I will."

Sidling past him into his office, she pressed her hands to her thighs to keep her floaty pink skirt from brushing up against him as she passed.

"You were skulking around out there," he explained after a beat of silence. Then he followed her deeper into the room, gesturing toward the two gray upholstered chairs in front of his desk. "I kept seeing a pink shadow flit past the glass."

"I'll try to keep future skulking to a minimum." She dropped into one of the chairs and was surprised when he took the one beside her instead of sitting behind his desk. "What did you want to meet with me about?"

Her pulse jackhammered at his nearness. He'd long ago ditched the jacket of the custom gray suit he'd worn at the photo shoot, leaving him in a well-cut black button-down shirt with no tie. The gray gabardine of the pants had a subtle weave shot through with navy threads, something she'd never have noticed if his knee wasn't just a hand's breadth from hers. He even smelled expensive—his aftershave was pleasantly smoky and appealing, yet so subtle she'd have to lean nearer to really get a handle on the scent notes.

Had she ever been so close to him? Her mouth felt a little dry, and she wished she had another mint. Instead, she swallowed hard while her gaze traveled up his broad chest to where square shoulders stretched the black cotton of his shirt. His chiseled square jaw gave him a determined air, and his high cheekbones were a gift from his breathtakingly lovely mother. His lips were full and sensuous. Not that she was thinking about them, exactly. More like trying not to.

She swallowed again.

"I have a problem that I hope you can help me with," Lucas began, his golden-brown eyes locked on hers.

She really hoped he hadn't noticed her ogling him.

"I'll do what I can." Folding her hands in her lap, she kept her expression agreeable. Professional. Unogling.

"Good." His jaw flexed, and his hand fisted where it rested on the arm of his chair. "Because I want your assistance locating a leak in the organization."

Her stomach dropped so fast she felt like she'd just fallen down an elevator shaft. Her heart rate accelerated. She blinked even though she wanted to remain perfectly still.

"A…leak?" she repeated, wondering if he'd learned she'd been approached by a competing firm.

She'd received the offer by phone, but perhaps someone had overheard. She hadn't done anything wrong, of course. There was no reason to feel a stab of guilt. No reason even to bring up the job offer she'd turned down since she most certainly was *not* the leak. Plus, she'd never looked into the legality of her former coworker's claim their conversation was still covered by her nondisclosure agreement with About Face, so she wasn't sure how much she could share, anyway.

Yet Lucas's watchful gaze felt intent. Intense, even. She swore she could feel it examine every single inch of her.

Heat rushed up the back of her neck. She could not afford to lose this job. Could not afford to have the Deschampses suspect her of spying.

"Yes. I think we have a spy in our midst, Blair." One dark eyebrow arched as his expression turned thoughtful. Musing. "Would you help me find the guilty party?"

Two

Lucas didn't want to miss any nuance of Blair's reaction.

Yet even though he'd intended to study her features for any trace of guilt, he somehow got distracted by the play of her slender fingers over the hem of her pink chiffon skirt just above her knees. One French-manicured fingertip absently traced the scalloped edging, drawing his attention to Blair's killer legs.

Sending his thoughts spiraling down a carnal path right up until the moment she spoke again.

"I'm not sure how you think I could help with a task like that." She spoke with crispness, her cool tone completely at odds with his overheated visions. "I have the shortest tenure of anyone in the company."

When his attention flicked up to her face, he saw only composure there. Any hope he'd had of catching a betraying expression had smoldered to ash under the weight of his desire for her. He'd lost an opportunity, but he still had every intention of going through with his plan. He needed to keep tabs on her activities, for one thing. And for another? She should be aware that he was watching her. Closely.

If Blair turned out to be the leak, she'd have to be more careful.

"Precisely why I think you're a good fit for the job." Lucas forced himself to lean back in his chair, putting more space between them in order to rein in his wayward longings. "You won't have preconceived notions about your coworkers."

She frowned, her rosebud lips pouting. "You don't, either, though, have you? According to the watercooler gossip I've heard, you've only joined the company to help your mother shore up the bottom line."

"The gossip is correct." He hauled his gaze away from her mouth to take in the sparsely decorated executive suite that had been requisitioned for his use for the upcoming weeks. He'd temporarily joined the business to help his mother's floundering company, but if Deschamps ended up being taken over by his father's conglomerate at the end of the month, Lucas wouldn't spend another day in this office. "I'm on the board of directors at Deschamps Cosmetics, but I don't technically work here. Yet when my mother asked for help stabilizing the business, I could hardly refuse her."

"So you wouldn't have preconceived notions about the people who work here any more than I would," she pointed out, folding her arms across her silky white blouse. "Why can't you do your own spying on the employees?"

If only it was that simple.

"Because I'm the founder's son. Juicy conversation grinds to a halt when I walk in a room." He leaned forward. "Whereas you will have access to more relaxed and honest discussions."

A shadow passed through her pale eyes, and she quickly glanced down. He became aware of how quiet the building had gone outside his office now that it was well after the end of the workday.

Heat pumped through him at the knowledge they were all alone on this floor. Just him, and this woman who fascinated him like no one else.

"I'd like to consider it before I give you my answer," Blair said finally, her voice softer. "Can I let you know at the end of the week?"

"Certainly." The meeting had gone better than he would have hoped. He'd been in a private room with her for five minutes and hadn't allowed his personal desire to decline their conversation into bickering. His sense of satisfaction in that prompted him to push his luck. "You can have until Saturday, in fact, when I'd like you to work on the photo shoot at my mother's brownstone."

She blinked at him. "You mean *my* brownstone? As in, where I live with my roommates?"

"Yes. *Banner* magazine is doing a piece on her for their notable-women-of-the-year issue," he reminded her, certain his mother must have talked to Blair and her roommates about the project already. "They want some photos of the Brooklyn apartment building she's donated to help women in creative fields afford to establish themselves in New York City."

Blair straightened in her seat, flipping her long ponytail off her shoulder as her chin jutted at him. "We do pay rent, you know. We're not taking handouts."

"Of course." He bent his head, acknowledging the mistake. He hadn't meant to wound her pride. "I only meant that she doesn't profit from the project. Anyway, my mother will mention Deschamps Cosmetics in the accompanying interview, and she insisted on using her own makeup and makeup artist."

Blair reared back at this. "I don't think she'll want the newest makeup artist on staff to do her face for something like that. She could call in anyone she wanted. I'm sure she has a personal preference."

Did she? Lucas realized he had no idea. Perhaps in distancing himself from his father over the years, he'd also unwittingly put more space between him and his mother. He should remedy that. Yet his instincts told him his ambitious mom would prefer to have Lucas's help maintaining control of her company, rather than maintaining control over who applied her makeup for a photo shoot.

Lucas needed to spend more time with Blair and having her work this job would allow him to do that.

"My mother doesn't hire anyone she doesn't believe in. It says a lot about your talent that she not only offered you one of the places in the brownstone, but that she also hired you to work for her company."

Of course, that would add a whole other level of betrayal to the Deschamps Cosmetics traitor if it turned out to be Blair. Because then she wasn't just deceiving her employer, she was also thumbing her nose at the whole competitive process to be chosen for a spot in the brownstone. Potential residents vied for acceptance by submitting résumés and essays about what they hoped to accomplish while in New York. Each candidate was reviewed by a small committee of his mother's friends, but the ultimate approval came from Cybil herself.

Considering what a blow it would be to his mother to discover one of her picks was selling company secrets, Lucas really hoped he was wrong about Blair.

Blowing out a long breath, she nodded. "All right. I'll do Cybil's makeup, assuming she wants me to. I'm flattered to be asked."

She shifted in her seat, the movement bringing her bare knee close to his. The tall heels of her rose-colored pumps disappeared in the thick weave of the dark Turkish rug beneath their feet. His attention moved slowly up her calves, where the muscles bunched, thanks to the way the shoes flexed her feet. His fingers itched to trace the same path.

Their eyes met. Held.

Lucas's pulse stirred.

Her pupils widened as she breathed faster, tiny puffs escaping her parted lips.

"If that's all?" She leaped to her feet, edging back a step to put more space between them.

Was she in a hurry to retreat because she felt the same draw as him? Or because of a guilty conscience? More time with her would help him ascertain the truth.

"Yes. That's all." He rose more slowly while she sidestepped toward the exit. "I'll look forward to your answer when I see you Saturday."

Her step faltered. Her skirt swung to a stop, the chiffon layers swaying into place around her thighs.

"You'll be there for the shoot?" Her gaze drifted south for a moment before snapping back up to his face.

He steeled himself against the impulse to reach for her and answer that feminine curiosity with some frank male interest of his own.

Instead, he simply nodded. "It's a significant publicity opportunity for her brand. *Banner* reaches a different demographic than we've targeted in the past."

"Good. That's…good." She practically lurched for the door. "I'll see you then."

Darting past him, Blair rushed out of his office. He caught a hint of vanilla in her wake, as if the scent of all the treats she baked clung to her full-time.

And while he resisted watching her walk away when he closed the door again, he couldn't quite hold back the urge to take a deep breath and catch that slight fragrance again. For reasons he couldn't fully identify, he wanted Blair with a hunger he hadn't felt for any woman in a long time.

But he'd be damned if he'd act on that until he knew for certain she wasn't the one selling company secrets.

"Woman, what has gotten into you?"

Blair glanced up at Tana Blackstone—one of her roommates—who was standing at the foot of the brownstone's stairs near the kitchen, where Blair poured a hot sauce over her pan of chocolate baklava. The aspiring actress must have had an audition today because the hair she normally dyed in rainbow-bright shades was its natural glossy brown. Even her clothes were subdued—a form-fitting black dress with a jean jacket thrown over it and a pair of gold hoops in her ears. Tana's regular style favored leather and spikes with a touch of glitter, so her out-fit was a far cry from her usual getup, although she still wore her favorite combat boots with the dress. At five foot three, Tana had a delicate prettiness that she rarely showed off, preferring a unique kind of armor over traditional beauty.

Tana scowled at her as she stalked into the kitchen, arms crossed.

"What's with the nonstop baking?" Tana picked up an empty pot and retrieved a clean spoon from the silverware drawer before helping herself to what-ever she could skim off the sides. "For three days straight, you've been like a woman possessed in here. I've never seen so many baked goods outside of a pastry shop."

Surprise, surprise, it had been three days ago that she'd had the meeting in Lucas's office. The one in which he'd told there was a spy in the office. It still made her gut clench to think about the open job offer from her former employer. The one her former boss had called about to peddle to her personally a few hours ago. Apparently her ex-colleague hadn't been the only one at About Face interested in trying to turn her into a spy. They'd upped the pressure.

Not that she wanted to dwell on it. Hence the bak-ing.

"Are you complaining?" Blair moved the tray of baklava to an out-of-the-way spot on the counter so she could continue stirring the dough for a batch of sugar cookies. "I thought you liked it when I bake."

"I do like it." Tana used one arm to lever herself up on the opposite counter of the kitchen. "But it doesn't take a genius in psychology to figure out you're working through some kind of obsessive-compulsive disorder. Or using cooking as an outlet for anxiety, maybe. Or possibly hiding from your life by spending every free moment in the kitchen."

The space was small, but it had been recently remodeled to make every inch functional, so even with Tana taking up a portion of the counter, Blair had room to work.

"That's a lot of possibilities," she observed dryly, "Maybe you need to be a psychology genius after all."

She blended the butter and sugar with a wooden spoon. She liked the high-end utensils, but she missed some of the implements she'd grown up with. The ones her mother had used when teaching her to bake. A pang of fear for her mother sliced through all the other emotions that had been swelling inside her this entire week.

"Faster for you to just tell me," Tana countered, pointing her spoon in Blair's direction. "Cheaper, too. I give reasonably good talk therapy."

Blair debated what to say. She needed a friend. But she didn't want to talk about Lucas. Although, compared to the anxiety about her mom threatening to carry her off like a riptide current, Blair wondered if sharing some of her Lucas angst made more sense. Her roommates already knew that Blair spent most of her weekends in the Catskills visiting with Amber, but they didn't know why.

She'd been relieved not to have to talk about it.

But now? A white-hot spear of worry stabbed her insides and she ached to share her concerns with someone.

"Oh, my God. What's wrong?" Tana slid off the countertop, allowing the pan and spoon to fall into the sink with a clatter as she kept her eyes on Blair. She wrapped a gentle hand around Blair's elbow. "Did I say something offensive? You know I'm just blathering, right? I know *nothing* about talk therapy. Nothing about anything. You should totally cook if it makes you happy."

Her friend's earnest concern eased a layer of Blair's fears. She set aside the mixing bowl, appreciating that someone in her life cared enough to question what was going on with her.

"You didn't offend me," Blair assured her, tipping her forehead briefly to Tana's. "You're awesome."

The praise made Tana reel back a little, flustering her.

"Well. I do try for maximum awesomeness." She shrugged a shoulder before her expression turned serious. "But are you deflecting? Because if something's wrong, I hope you know you can tell me."

Blair wondered, not for the first time, what life circumstances had shaped Tana. She could present a jaded side as often as she wanted to the world, but Blair knew there was a deep empathy within. She'd watched Tana wield an old-time camcorder around the brownstone sometimes, filming minute details of their lives—Blair cleaning her makeup brushes in the sink, or Sable shortening a hem on a dress—in a way that felt personal. Intimate, even.

Blair was about to speak, to share some of what was going on with her mother, when the door to the apartment opened on the floor above them.

"Please say we're doing Friday-night happy hour!" a familiar voice called down the stairs as a set of keys rattled and clunked to the floor. Tennis shoes bounded down the steps toward the kitchen. "I know I can't drink, but I have a serious pregnancy craving for popcorn and girl talk. Although I also want whatever I can smell baking down here—"

Sable Cordero, a fashion stylist and their roommate who now spent many nights with her boss after a surprise pregnancy, paused at the bottom of the stairs as she came into view. Dressed in winter-white trousers and a matching tunic with an oyster-colored shawl sweater draped over her shoulders, Sable's clothes made a dramatic backdrop for her rich spill of raven hair, which had only grown longer and thicker in the last few months. She glowed with all those expectant-mama hormones.

"I interrupted something," Sable announced, her hazel eyes bouncing back and forth between them as she stepped deeper into the kitchen. "What did I miss?"

Tana looped her arm through Blair's. "This one was about to tell me why she's obsessively baking all the time. Let's sit around the table and I'll pop the popcorn. You make Blair start talking before she loses her nerve."

"Done." Sable stepped in front of them to pull out one of the white dining-room chairs with gray twill cushions. "Put her in the hot seat."

Blair dutifully sat under the combined influence of her friends' directions. "I would gladly make the popcorn," she protested. "You know I like being in charge of the happy hour snacks."

Although she had forgotten about their tradition tonight since her thoughts were scattered all over the place with her worries about Lucas, his request that she help him find the spy and her mother facing most of her chemo treatments alone.

"And we like giving back to you sometimes." Sable dragged one of the dining-room chairs back from the table and then slid another one in front of it. She then slipped off her tennis shoes to sit in the first seat while putting her feet up on the second. "I owe you a lot for helping me work things out with Roman. So if you're having trouble now, I wish you'd give me the chance to lend a hand in return."

Touched, Blair smiled at her friend while popcorn kernels started to erupt in the next room.

Tana leaned over the kitchen counter that adjoined the dining room. "I can hear, too," she announced. "Tell us what's going on, Blair. Does it have to do with Lucas Deschamps?"

Blair supposed she shouldn't be surprised at the guess since Lucas had been to the brownstone before. No doubt her roommates had read something into their sort-of animosity toward each other.

"Honestly, he's a problem for another day." Like tomorrow. When she had to decide whether or not she was going to help him find the mole inside Deschamps Cosmetics. *After* she found a way to explain that she'd been approached for that exact task. Tonight, all Blair's thoughts were in the Catskill Mountains with her mother. She dragged in a deep breath. "I'm more worried about my mom right now. You know I take the train most weekends to see her?"

Tana nodded while the microwave chimed behind her, the scent of popcorn mingling with the fragrant melted butter wafting from the stovetop.

"Is she sick?" Sable asked, leaning forward and resting her elbows on the table.

"She has ovarian cancer." She struggled to say the words in a normal voice and not whisper the dreaded *cancer* word like the coward she was inside. Whisper or shout, the diagnosis brought frightening consequences either way. "Stage IIc. She was really fortunate to discover it when she did."

For an instant, both Tana and Sable stared at her, unblinking. Frozen with the unexpected news.

But then, Blair knew firsthand how terrifying that kind of disclosure could be. A moment later, Sable moved toward her, murmuring consoling words as she hooked an arm around Blair's shoulders. The touch steadied her.

"Her doctors are hopeful," she reminded herself, grateful to feel Sable's hand slide over hers, even as her friend shifted to meet her gaze. "They felt good about the surgery to remove…well, everything related to her ovaries."

Tana left the kitchen, leaving the snack behind to take the seat across the table from Sable. Blair's friends flanked her, their concern clear from their expressions.

"So she's recovering now?" Tana's gaze flicked from Blair to Sable and then back again.

"She's having chemotherapy. There's a good facility up there, and I rented her a cabin in the woods that's near one of her old friends who can drive her to the appointments. Mom had said she wanted to be closer to the mountains. It was one of the things she wished for when she—" Her breath caught, another stab of hurt robbing her voice. "She made a bucket list. And living near the mountains was on it."

"Oh, honey." Sable left her chair again to throw

her arms around Blair's neck. "I'm sorry she's going through this. It must be so hard for you not to be with her."

Tana's gaze was steady. "How can we help? Do you want company next time you make the trip to see her? Or can we do something here to free you up to visit longer?"

Tears burned the backs of Blair's eyes at the outpouring of support. Both Sable's warmth of spirit and Tana's practical goodwill meant the world to her. She hadn't realized until just this moment how lonely she'd been, how often she'd turned to her mother for encouragement.

"I don't need help, beyond a place to vent," she assured them, knowing she was already doing everything in her power to make ends meet. Everything ethical, at least. "I think I just needed this. Some friend love. And to, you know, share the hurt."

"Of course you did." Leaning back to peer into Blair's eyes, Sable rubbed a comforting hand along her shoulder. "That's what friends are for. Talk to us whenever things worry you. It's like sharing a heavy burden. You need to let others help you lighten the load."

They spoke for a little while longer about the particulars of her mom's illness and response to her therapy, then Sable retreated to the kitchen to retrieve food and drinks.

Blair picked up her phone to scroll through her

playlists to find the right tunes to send to the Blue-tooth speaker. And as the Latin pop music played—by a new artist she'd heard about from Antonia, the volleyball player at her last makeup job—Blair re-alized that Sable had been right. She did feel a little better for having shared her burdens. At least for the moment.

Tana leaned over the table, lowering her voice. "I hope you know that Sable and I will be there for you tomorrow if you need us to run interference with Lucas during the photo shoot."

And just that fast, reality crashed back in on Blair's lightened mood.

Tomorrow she needed to give Lucas an answer to his request. But did she have to confess that she'd been tapped for spying when she'd done nothing of the sort?

What if he didn't believe her when she said she'd refused the job? She couldn't afford to lose her po-sition here.

"You'll be there?" Blair finally responded, her dis-tracted thoughts sucking her into a whirlwind of doubt.

"Of course. The *Banner* magazine piece is all about Cybil's efforts to resurrect the club residence for women in New York City." Tana winked. "We're the chosen lucky ones, so they want all three of us in a photo. Didn't you see the invitation from the re-porter in your email? We might even be interviewed."

"I must have missed it," Blair murmured as Sable

brought in a silver tray filled with two margarita glasses and one water bottle and set it down in the middle of the table with a flourish.

"Well, just know we've got your back with Lucas," Tana continued, retrieving one of the margarita glasses.

Blair grabbed the other one, very ready for a hit of tequila to take the rough edges off this day. For tonight, at least, she'd enjoy this time with her girlfriends.

Because when tomorrow came and Lucas demanded an answer of her, she didn't have any clue how she could possibly refuse.

Three

"Blair is turning out to be an incredible asset to Deschamps Cosmetics, isn't she?" Lucas's mother remarked as she joined him in the enclosed garden outside the Brooklyn brownstone, site of the shoot for *Banner* magazine.

Lucas turned from watching the photographer reposition Blair and her roommates on the garden's gray wicker patio furniture. They'd saved this outdoor shot for last, shooting during the peak of the golden hour before sunset. Lucas stood on the periphery of the makeshift set, while a stylist, makeup artist, hair designer and two camera assistants filled out the rest of the semicircle around the three current residents of the brownstone, who were being grouped in a variety of ways. The women all wore fitted silk dresses designed by Marcel Zayn, the fashion house where resident Sable Cordero worked, and where the father of her future child, Roman Zayn, served as CEO.

Blair, in particular, looked stunning in the ice-blue one-shoulder dress that clung to her curves, the rosy hue of sunlight making her skin glow. Lucas had a hard time looking away from her, but he did so now to glance at his tall, regal mother as she smiled with obvious pride in the young women. He questioned how much to share with her about Blair. Cybil Deschamps might be a force to reckon with in New York society and the business world alike, but Lucas knew a softer side of her. A very human side that would surely be crushed to think someone she'd championed for a spot in the brownstone, and a place on her staff, might have an ulterior motive. Better to keep quiet about his suspicions until he knew more.

"Blair is very talented," Lucas answered his mother honestly. "And she did a great job on your makeup, Mom. You look beautiful."

Approaching seventy, his elegant mother had always appeared much younger than her years. In the last decade she'd taken to more noninvasive surgical treatments, but she hadn't needed them. Her wintry blond hair worked well with some gray in it, and she'd always worn it cut just above her shoulders.

Keen blue eyes missed nothing when it came to her company, although she had overlooked his father's affairs in the years she'd labored hard to make her business a success. Lucas had always regretted not outing the old man sooner, but he'd hung on to the delusion of winning his father's approval for far too long.

"She did. I will confess I had Roger review it for me when she finished." She nodded toward the senior makeup artist on the shoot who was standing with the hair designer near the patio door. "Just to make sure he thought it was calibrated correctly for the lighting, but to my eyes, it was nicely done." She pivoted away from the photo shoot to meet Lucas's eyes. "I hear she donates a lot of free time on weekends doing makeup for patients at a cancer-treatment center in the Catskills. She's really very sweet."

"She does?" Lucas frowned, the image not fitting with his idea of Blair as a potential corporate spy. Then again, it fit with his sense that she seemed a little too good to be true. "Where did you hear that?"

His mother gave a light shrug, fluffing her hair. "I don't remember, darling. From one of the interns, maybe? They all adore her for the homemade things she brings into the office." She beamed up at him. "Have you tried her chocolate baklava? It's positively sinful."

No surprise that his mother was a Blair devotee. Cybil had called Blair a clear favorite from the first time she'd read her résumé for a spot in the brown-stone.

And while Lucas could admit now that she was talented, he still didn't trust Blair's sweet side. The story about providing free makeup sessions to cancer patients could easily be watercooler talk meant to divert attention from Blair's real objective. The fact that she did the so-called gratis work far from the five boroughs made him doubt it all the more.

He was still brooding over this new piece of the Blair mystery when his mother laid a hand on his arm.

"Did you want to get dinner after the shoot? Review our strategy to win over the necessary board support?"

The invitation pulled a smile from him in spite of his dark speculating. Even when he'd been a kid, his mom had made time for him no matter how much business called her.

"We both know the strategy inside and out." They'd been discussing this for weeks, refining their plan almost daily to ensure they could show tangible proof that Deschamps would increase profits considerably by the first quarter of the new year. "Between the new product launch, the increased online shopping outlets and the marketing campaign, we're a lock to persuade enough board members to vote against selling to DLH."

Assuming no one sold out their secret initiatives

to competitors who could steal an advantage from them. Anger flashed through him as his attention darted back to Blair, where she was trading places with one of the other women, the photographer working quickly to get as many shots as possible while the outdoor lighting was favorable. He'd thought about her far too often this week and looked forward to seeing her after the shoot in spite of all his doubts about her.

And no matter his personal feelings, it made good sense to keep an eye on her for the weeks before the board meeting. The buyout offer was attractive, and several board members had argued strongly in favor of accepting it. But if Lucas and Cybil could demonstrate enough promise in the new fiscal year, they had at least two other board members who'd suggested they would be willing to vote against the sale of Deschamps to DLH Luxe International, a publicly traded company owned by Peter Deschamps.

Until the vote, Lucas couldn't afford to relax his guard.

When his mother spoke again her tone was serious. Quiet. "You know, I wouldn't hold it against you if you wanted the sale to happen. DLH Luxe will belong to you one day, anyway."

"I have my own business. I don't need his." He'd been adamant with his father that he didn't want the role. His dad had daughters from his first marriage—Lucas's half sisters. The business could go to them.

Should go to them, in fact. "And even if I wanted DLH, that has no bearing on this. You're keeping Deschamps Cosmetics. It's your business, not his."

She smiled up at him just as the photographer declared the shoot a wrap for the day.

"You're a good son. And we could have dinner without talking business, you know." She kissed him lightly on the cheek.

"Any other time I would, but I'm meeting with Blair." He caught the gleam in his mother's eye and quickly added, "About business."

"I'm sure." Cybil smiled at him as the shoot began to break up, the participants gathering items to pack up for the day while the roommates trooped back into the brownstone. "*Business*. Enjoy yourself, darling. We'll talk more on Monday."

He restrained further comment, knowing she'd gotten the wrong impression. But better that his mother thought he was hitting on one of her employees than that she knew the truth.

That he was trying to find out who was spying on the company she'd built from the ground up, and that there was a chance it could be Blair.

She wasn't hiding from Lucas, exactly.

Seated at the small home desk inside her third-floor bedroom after the photoshoot, Blair withdrew her phone to text her mom. She realized her sexy, brooding boss was surely waiting for her downstairs, expecting an answer about helping him find the spy in his company. But she could delay joining him for another few minutes.

She had already changed from the gorgeous silk gown Sable had loaned her to a lightweight summer dress and sandals. Her hair remained pinned up from when she'd washed her face of the photo makeup. A warm breeze blew through her bedroom window as she opened her messaging app, and Blair breathed in the roselike fragrance of the honey locust tree in bloom right outside. Who would have guessed such a sweetly decadent scent could permeate the air on a Brooklyn street?

She wished her mother was here to enjoy it with her. The pang in her chest remained as she typed: I finished my work for the day. I could still get the 8:30 train so I can be there to make you breakfast!

Part of her wondered if a better daughter would just hop on the train and show up, whether she'd been summoned or not. But she respected her mother's independence, too, and understood that not everyone was comforted by social time when they felt ill. So she waited.

You know I love seeing you, but how about a raincheck this weekend? Still tired.

Defeat made her shoulders slump so hard that she felt close to tears. Because of worry about her mom?

Or from not feeling needed? Or had she hoped the trip to see her mother would somehow excuse her skipping out on the meeting with Lucas?

The possibility forced her to recognize she needed to take more ownership for her choices so she wouldn't feel so guilty about the offer from her former employer. She'd been firm with the *colleague* who kept dangling the possibility of a fat paycheck in front of her. Yet part of her kept hoping About Face would still give her some freelance assignments since she'd worked hard for them. She didn't wish to cut ties. But that didn't mean she needed to feel guilty for an offer she hadn't accepted. She would go to the meeting with Lucas with a clear conscience.

Okay. Rest well, then, and I'll see you next weekend for sure. I love you, Mom.

A moment later, her mother sent an animated fish blowing bubbles and kisses toward her. She smiled at the silly character until there was a soft knock at her door. Her breath caught.

But then the sound was followed by Sable's voice. "Blair?"

"Come in," she answered, swiping a finger under one eye to hide a tear and grateful it hadn't been Lucas at the door. Despite her pep talk with herself, she wasn't quite ready to face him. "I'm bagging up the clothes right now."

She stood and strode toward her closet to retrieve the loaned garments while Sable stepped through the door, leaving it open behind her. Her four-months-pregnant friend wore a boho cotton tunic over capri pants, her look as chic as ever.

"I'm in no hurry for the dresses. I just wanted to check on you since we couldn't really talk downstairs," Sable insisted, her sandals slapping lightly along the floor. "How's your mother today? Is she going to let you visit?"

Retrieving a garment bag with the Zayn Designs logo printed on it, Blair shook her head. "She says she's tired. But we made a plan for next weekend."

Another light knock behind them announced Tana stepping into the room. She carried a garment bag that matched the one Blair was zipping closed. Tana laid hers on Blair's bed. Tana had added pink strands to her hair again. Now that the photos were finished for the day, she was back in ripped black skinny jeans, studded boots and a crop top with a butterfly.

"You're not going to the Catskills after all?" Tana asked, knowing well that Blair had been hoping her mom would change her mind after their visit the night before.

Shaking her head, Blair pressed the air out of her bag before laying it on top of Tana's. "No. As much as I like seeing my mom every weekend, I know sometimes when you're sick you just want to be alone."

Before her friends could reply, a familiar masculine voice rumbled from the hallway.

"Blair?"

Lucas stood framed in the open door, his broad shoulders filling out the gray blazer he wore open over a pale blue button-down and dark jeans. Blair's breath snagged at the sight of him, her heartbeat skipping in a purely feminine reaction that—for a moment—blocked out everything else.

But only for a moment. The expectant lift of one of his dark eyebrows reminded her he was there for business. Demanding a reply she'd promised.

"Are you ready to meet?" he continued, his voice somehow stirring her insides and making her nervous at the same time. "I thought we could use the rooftop garden, where we won't be interrupted."

"I'm ready," she assured him with more calmness than she felt. Then, turning to her friends, she said, "I'd better finish up my work for the day. Thanks again for loaning us the dresses, Sable. They really looked beautiful."

Sable leaned in for a hug. "Of course. I'll see you Friday night, if you're around."

Tana hugged her, too, which was a little bit of a surprise, until Tana used the contact as an excuse to whisper in her ear. "Sorry, I didn't see him coming."

The comment almost made her smile, a throwback to Tana's insistence that she'd run interference for her. As if anyone could prevent the consequences of her twisty work drama.

"I've got this," Blair whispered back before she let go.

Then, joining Lucas in the hallway, she walked up the stairs with him to the top floor of the brownstone, where an enclosed staircase led to the roof. His presence behind her was a shivery warmth at her back, awareness of him increasing with every step.

They hadn't spoken much today, even though he'd been present for most of the photo session around the brownstone. It occurred to her now that he'd been so quiet, in fact, that they hadn't engaged in their usual verbal sparring. She missed it, she realized.

"You didn't find one thing to criticize during the shoot today," she observed as she stepped out onto the rooftop patio.

Broad plank flooring gave way to plants and small trees around the perimeter, the greenery providing natural walls that made the spot feel private though the neighborhood below them was alive with pedestrians enjoying the good weather. White lights were strung in the small trees, illuminating the central seating area, where two outdoor couches with plump taupe cushions faced one another, a low teakwood table between them. A bottle of champagne was chilling in a silver bucket, a tray with glasses beside it.

"I wasn't in charge," he said simply, gesturing to

one of the couches. "Today the spotlight was on my mother, and it was her moment to shine."

"Are we celebrating?" she asked as she took a seat, caught off guard by the sight of the champagne on top of Lucas's uncharacteristic agreeable mood.

"I certainly hope so. A successful editorial piece, for one. And your acquiescence to help me, for another." He took the seat beside her, leaving a space between them that was just a little narrower than was strictly professional, but he didn't crowd her, either.

Her pulse galloped faster.

"How very…confident of you." She watched as he tugged the excellent vintage from the ice bucket, his expensive watch glinting in the fairy lights overhead.

How would she handle this conversation? What if admitting that she'd been tapped by her former employer stirred Lucas's suspicions about her? He could have her position terminated. And even if he didn't take that approach, he could ensure her spot in the brownstone was revoked. Either way, a retaliatory move from this powerful man would eliminate any hope she had of paying for her mother's therapy.

"In truth, one of my mother's friends sent the champagne to her today, but since she doesn't drink, I thought we might as well enjoy it. Although I stand by what I said." He popped the top expertly, not spilling a drop before filling her glass and passing the flute to her. "I hope we'll have a new partnership to celebrate."

Blair watched the bubbles fizz, reminding her of the silly fish character her mother had sent her. Thoughts of her mom underscored that Blair could not afford a misstep tonight. She couldn't risk alienating Lucas or losing the financial security of this job.

"I think we will," she replied softly, signing on to the only viable way forward through this mess. She *wanted* to find out who would try and undermine Deschamps Cosmetics, she realized. She believed in the company. "Because I've decided to help you."

Lucas finished filling his own glass before turning toward her.

"You'll work with me to find out who's selling out company secrets?"

A shiver tripped over her skin under his steady regard.

She licked dry lips. "I will."

Though his gaze never left her, he gently tipped his crystal champagne flute to hers, the clear tone ringing in the summer night. Sealing her fate as his collaborator in this.

"In that case, cheers to a new partnership." He lifted his glass and drank deeply, the strong column of his throat flexing.

Blair sipped more carefully, studying him surreptitiously over the rim of her glass. Her gaze dipped from his neck to the hint of bronzed skin visible in the open top button of his shirt. Then lower, following the line of buttons down the front of his shirt, the crisp cotton fitted close to a body she'd observed often enough to know was well-defined. Leanly muscular.

What would it have been like to meet him outside of the job she desperately needed? A man who sacrificed his valuable professional time to help his mother stabilize her own business. After all, was his position that much different than her own, doing anything to help a parent?

"Do you have a strategy in mind?" she asked, setting aside the glass to keep this night from feeling too friendly. She should learn what he wanted from her and walk away before the champagne and appeal of the man went to her head.

"I did." He set his glass on the teak table, his forearm briefly brushing her knee through the thin fabric of her summer dress.

"Past tense?" she asked, resisting the urge to smooth over the spot with her hand, as if she could erase the way contact with him sparked sensations all through her. "Meaning you no longer have a strategy?"

"I'm concerned my plan might not be viable since it involved working on the weekends." Leaning back into the overstuffed cushions, he shifted so he could see her while draping one arm along the back of the sofa, close to her neck.

With the warmth of his fingers so close to the

bared skin beneath the low knot of her casually gathered hair, it took Blair a minute to understand the
significance of his words.

"Weekends," she repeated, heart falling at the
potential problems that wrought. She grabbed her
champagne flute again, clutching the stem of her
glass more tightly. "I see."

"Excuse me for overhearing your comment to
your friends today, but it sounds like you're spending your weekends visiting an ill relative."

How quickly her worlds had collided when she
wanted to keep them far apart from one another. Not
that it should matter since she was doing all this for
her mom. She just hadn't been ready to share something so personal with him.

Now she didn't see a choice.

"I do. That is, I have been traveling to see my
mother as many weekends as possible, but if that
conflicts with what you're asking of me, I can figure
out another way to spend time with her."

"Blair." His tone was admonishing, his hand resting for the briefest moment on her shoulder. "What
kind of monster do you take me for?"

She turned to look him in the eye, and his touch
vanished. Which was surely for the best. Yet her
whole body lit up from within, coming alive as if all
her atoms were doing pirouettes at the same time.

She opened her lips to answer, but his tawny eyes
fastened on her mouth and made her forget whatever

she'd been about to say. The night sounds of traffic and a noisy dinner party in the next building over were welcome distractions to keep her from falling deeper under Lucas Deschamps's spell.

"We'll readjust the plan to make sure you can still visit her." He paused a moment, eyes curious, and she guessed he was waiting for her to say more about it. When she didn't, he continued. "There's an industry conference in Miami ten days from now. Deschamps is sponsoring several employees to attend."

Straightening, her professional curiosity got the better of her. "I know. I was disappointed I missed the application process."

"You'll attend as my guest." He leaned forward again, reaching into the champagne bucket to refresh their drinks.

Blair was surprised to discover she must have finished her first one in a fit of nerves. She passed him her glass, and his thumb glanced along hers.

"You're going?" She hadn't been expecting any of this—Lucas's kindness in not wanting to thwart her visits to her mother, or his plan of action involving traveling together.

She'd never felt so off balance, and it didn't have anything to do with the champagne.

"Yes. I'm especially interested in the group from Deschamps who will be attending, so I'd like to have you involved, being my ears and eyes among them." When he handed her back the flute, he held it an extra moment, so that they both touched the crystal, fingers overlapping. "I'm trusting you, Blair."

Her heart jackhammered with a confusing mixture of guilt and awareness. She didn't know how to read him, yet she couldn't help feeling like maybe he read her all too well.

"I hope so." The words spilled out of their own volition, a foolish wish. Her fingers tightened around his in an effort to win the flute, but she only succeeded in tipping it toward her, sloshing a bit of champagne onto her dress. "That is, I wouldn't think you'd ask me to do this if you didn't trust me a little."

"Sorry about that," he muttered, frowning down at the skirt. He withdrew a folded white square from an interior pocket of his jacket and used the cloth—a handkerchief—she realized belatedly, to blot at the spilled drink.

As she watched him tend to the small spot on her thigh, using only gentlemanly care, a lightning bolt of desire sizzled through her so rapidly she nearly clenched her legs together to ease the sudden ache.

She must have gasped. Or gulped. Or made some sound that caught his attention, because Lucas's hand stilled. His attention shifted from her dress to her face, where his keen eyes seemed to pull every last carnal thought from her head. Because what else could account for the way his pupils widened? The way his nostrils flared, and jaw tightened?

His breathing grew deep and heavy, his chest close enough for her to observe every fascinating shift.

"You should tell me to leave now, Blair." His words were a growled command she refused to obey.

The air between them felt charged. Hot. Alive with possibility.

She'd never experienced this kind of draw to someone. The force of it was so potent she couldn't fathom how to ignore the feeling. His hand still hovered above her thigh, where he'd abandoned the task of cleaning her up. And at this moment, with all her awareness centered on her leg, where he'd caressed her through her dress, Blair couldn't do anything but follow the pull of attraction.

"Touch me." She hardly recognized her own voice as she issued a command of her own. Wanton. Needy. But absolutely certain. "Please, Lucas. Touch me again."

Four

Lucas had a litany of reasons he should have refused.

Hell, he'd *asked her* to turn him away so he could find the will to leave tonight. But he didn't stand a chance of fighting himself and her, too. Not when she looked like his every fantasy coming to life, her full lips shaping words he'd secretly craved.

The city disappeared around them, the nearest rooftops dark while theirs remained wreathed in decorative trees and white lights to shield them from the rest of the world. He could touch her. Taste her. No one else would see. No one but his conscience would protest.

And since when did he rationalize bad decisions?

"Blair." He spoke her name with tenderness when he'd intended it to be a warning.

The sound only spurred her to reach for his hand. Taking it in hers, she lowered his palm to where he had rested it earlier.

To the middle of her thigh.

Even if the feel of her slim leg through the cotton dress hadn't persuaded him, the way Blair jolted at the contact cemented his fate. Her soft, startled gasp told him how much she liked the contact. And damn it to hell and back, he did, too.

Touch me.

Her words whispered through his brain, circling around until he was dizzy with the need to do exactly as she wished. He refused to think past this moment. Instead, he held her gaze while he walked his fingers along her thigh, gathering the fabric of her dress as he did so, slowly raising the hem.

Lashes fluttering, she tipped back her head, breaking eye contact. What a picture she made, the delectable expanse of her throat exposed while she gave herself over to his hands. Trusting him to make her feel good.

His blood surged hot, his every impulse centered around her. Finally, he dipped his gaze to the bare skin of her knees and the place where he was clenching her skirt in his fist. Every beat of his heart urged him closer to taking everything he wanted, the heavy thudding a vibration that rattled away his restraint and demanded he lose himself in her.

Easing his grip on her dress, he laid the material to one side of her, freeing his hand to settle on her naked thigh. He teased a touch up the outside of her calf, the muscle trembling and flexing under the caress. It wasn't enough.

He knew that, but still he moved slowly, half-fearing one of them would wake from whatever seductive spell the night had cast on them. He didn't want to stop touching her. So he cataloged every shift in her breathing and every nuance of expression as he trailed his fingers over the front of her leg, then dipped to the warmth of her inner thigh.

Her lips parted when he touched her there, her chest rising and falling faster with her accelerated breathing. The phenomenon continued as he inched higher. Higher. Until he was powerless to stop himself from looking down. Seeing his hand between her legs, his fingertip a mere inch from the peach-colored lace that hid her from view.

Her hand scrabbled against his chest, seeking purchase, a small mewling sound escaping her throat. Urging him on? Or cursing him for not moving faster? The sultry noise she made enflamed him as much as the silken feel of her skin or the unforgettable sight of that peach lace.

"Lucas." She breathed his name through parted

lips, her head snapping up and eyes opening to fix him with her gaze. "I ache."

Instantly, he altered his course, charged with easing that hurt. Fueled by the need to give her pleasure.

He didn't think. He simply swept her out of her seat and onto his lap, draping her over him. Her hip nudged an erection of epic proportion, but he stifled his own need to focus on hers. She wanted this ache gone—an ache he wanted to think he was responsible for—and he wouldn't rest until he'd accomplished that.

"I'll take care of you," he promised, his voice like gravel as he anchored her to him with one arm and nudged her thighs apart with the other. "But in return, you have to kiss me."

She stared down at him with passion-fogged eyes for a moment, then gave the slightest nod. Her vanilla scent surrounded him as the curtain of her hair fell alongside his face, her mouth teasing softly over his. The sweetness of the chaste kiss seemed at odds with her bold insistence that he touch her, but he could hardly complain when just the feel of those full lips against his was a potent aphrodisiac.

For a moment, he simply absorbed the feel of her, letting her find her way while he palmed the peach lace between her thighs. She sighed into him, her lips parting, her body molding to his. His restraint vanished at the feel of her straining to get close to him, her panties already so wet the lace clung to her.

It took a second for him to realize the feral growl vibrating the air was a sound he was making. But damn, he wanted to rip away their clothes. Lay her down. Cover her—

The metal door to the rooftop patio scraped open nearby.

"Blair?"

The sound of her friend's voice cut through the night, a slice of white light from the hall behind her casting the woman in shadow.

Blair slid off his lap at the same time Lucas cursed the timing. And maybe himself for letting things go so far.

"Yes?" Blair rose unsteadily to her feet, smoothing down the skirt of her dress. "Is everything okay?"

The other woman—Tana—marched toward them in her dark combat boots and ripped leggings, edging past the potted trees toward the seating area. She didn't spare him a glance, keeping her focus on her friend as she set aside an old-fashioned camcorder that she'd been carrying in one hand. She held a phone in the other.

"Your phone's been going crazy," she explained to Blair, holding out the still-vibrating device as she closed the gap between them. "I didn't mean to be nosy, but it looks like your mom's friend has been texting and calling nonstop."

"Oh, no." The quiet desperation in Blair's voice reminded Lucas of the conversation she hadn't wanted to have with him earlier. Her mother was obviously ill.

Seriously so?

Instinctively, he rose to stand beside Blair, his palm resting between her shoulder blades. Steadying her.

The other woman's attention shot to the gesture, not missing a thing. For a second, she narrowed her eyes at him. Assessing. Warning.

But then she stroked a comforting hand along Blair's arm.

"Want me to stay?" Tana asked her. "We can rent a car, you know, and drive up there tonight. I've been wanting to shoot some video in a setting outside the city."

Lucas told himself it was not his business. That Blair hadn't confided in him, and that he should allow her privacy to handle whatever was happening. But touching her, kissing her, and even feeling her tremble right now as she scrolled through her messages all brought out his every protective instinct. He wasn't about to let her drive anywhere while she was shaken and upset.

"I can take you," he offered, drawing her closer to lend whatever comfort his touch might provide.

He would have said more, but Tana frowned at him over Blair's shoulder. Should he have refrained from putting his time and vehicle at her disposal? Blair should know she had options, damn it.

"I should call her back," Blair said softly. "Excuse me."

Stepping away from them both, Blair strode to the edge of the rooftop patio, where dwarf trees lined the short wall between buildings. Lucas's gaze followed her until the woman beside him spoke.

"There's no need for you to stay," Tana Blackstone informed him flatly, folding her arms over the glittery butterfly shirt she wore. A pink rhinestone nose stud winked in the white lights as she frowned at him. "I'll make sure she gets wherever she needs to go tonight."

Lucas had no idea what he'd done to warrant the borderline hostile tone she took with him, but everything about the woman's body language suggested she'd prefer to push him over the side of the roof than see him remain with Blair any longer.

"I have no doubt you would," he returned easily, trying to recall what he knew about this resident of his mother's brownstone. An aspiring actress who'd lived all over the United States with an interest in film. No family to speak of—or at least, none that she'd claimed on her application to live there. And talented as hell. His mom had been so impressed with the audition tape Tana had submitted as part of her creative portfolio, she'd texted a snippet of it to Lucas. But he didn't think the woman was acting now. The glare she gave him felt authentic enough. "But if Blair is having problems in her family, it might be nice for her to feel supported by multiple friends."

Tana's eyes narrowed. She spoke in a low tone even though Blair stood far from them. "Is that what you are now? Her *friend*?"

"Do you have a problem with that?" he shot back, losing patience with her when he wanted to keep his attention on Blair.

Tana shook her head. "Not at all. But things looked more than friendly when I walked out here a minute ago. Especially considering she works for you."

Her words brought back the memory of Blair's breathless whimpers and hungry kisses. No question, things had spiraled out of control in a hurry.

"She works for my mother's company. Not mine," he clarified.

"Split hairs much?" she whispered in an aggressive tone, while they each kept an eye on Blair. "She's going through a lot right now. No need to complicate things by offering a *friendship* you don't intend to keep."

He wanted to argue that point, but how could he when he had no idea where things were headed between him and Blair? Instead, he tried to frame a way to ask about her mother's illness, but before he had the chance to do so, Blair stabbed a button on her phone and pivoted to face them.

"Mom is okay," she began, the words at odds with

her pale face as she walked toward them. "She fell and hit her head, but Valerie doesn't think she needs stitches."

"Should we head up there?" Tana asked at the same time Lucas said, "I can take you to see her."

Blair paused, glancing back and forth between them. A tiny furrow appeared between her eyebrows.

"Valerie convinced me to wait until the morning." She tucked her phone into a pocket of her sundress. "I'll take the train then and spend the day with Mom."

Lucas waited a moment, hoping Tana would retreat so he could speak to Blair privately for a bit longer, but her friend seemed glued to her side, slipping her arm through Blair's and tipping her head against Blair's shoulder. A silent show of comfort that made the line between Blair's eyebrows vanish.

A reminder that it wasn't his role to offer support to Blair. The kiss they'd shared had scrambled his brain and made him forget his real role where she was concerned. He needed to find out if she was spying on Deschamps Cosmetics, not fantasize about scenarios where he might touch her again.

He was quickly losing his objectivity with her, and that was unacceptable.

"I should be on my way." Shoving his hands in his pockets—all the better to prevent himself from pulling her against him—Lucas took a step back. "I hope tomorrow finds your mother well."

"Lucas, wait." Straightening from where she stood with her friend, Blair bit her lip as she studied him. "I'll walk out with you."

Mom is okay.
Mom is okay.

Blair hoped if she repeated it enough times her heart rate would slow down, so she let the reassuring words circle through her head the whole time she trekked down the brownstone's staircase with Lucas behind her. She'd flown into panic mode when Tana found them on the roof tonight, her gut twisting with a sickening fear that her mother could be—

Mom is okay, she told herself sternly as they reached the parlor floor and headed out onto the street. Only then did she allow herself to face Lucas.

In front of her stoop, she leaned a hip on the stone base of the handrail and allowed her gaze to roam over his too-handsome features. Golden-brown eyes tracked hers, seeming to read her mood even though she hadn't shared much with him about her mom. She was grateful he hadn't asked questions when she wasn't ready to share that piece of herself with him. Bad enough she'd shared an unwise kiss.

That she'd basically *demanded* he touch her.

She groaned at the memory. "So, about what happened upstairs. I know that I was out of line to, um, incite the kissing—"

"Whoa." Lucas pressed his thumb to her lips, gently

silencing her before he lowered his hand again. "I'm going to stop you right there, because if lines were crossed, it happened by mutual consent."

Her heart pounded faster from the contact, her mouth tingling. She waited to speak again while a young family passed, a studious-looking blond father pushing a stroller with a sleeping toddler, while the tall Latina woman next to him carried an infant strapped to her chest. The baby's head bobbed with each of the mother's steps, the adults sharing a laugh as they passed Blair's stoop.

Their side of the street quieted in the family's wake, although some noise from Fort Greene Park drifted on the breeze. A shrill whistle. A street singer accompanied by a lone guitar. Traffic spilling out onto nearby DeKalb Avenue. But here, on a residential sidewalk, their conversation felt private enough. Blair dragged in a breath sweetened with the fragrant honey locust flowers from the tree nearby, steeling herself for an awkward conversation.

"Okay. So what happened was mutual," she conceded, her cheeks warming with the memory of his hand beneath her dress. "I'm hoping a commitment to not letting it happen again will also be mutual."

Because things were already extremely screwed up between her and Lucas. She'd refused to spy on him. And he'd seemed suspicious of her, yet he'd asked her to help find the spy. She didn't know what to think. But she knew she had to keep her job and her spot in the brownstone while she continued to search for a secondary gig that would generate the rest of the funds she needed to pay her mother's bills. She'd do whatever it took to ensure her mother kept receiving treatment.

"Are you sure that's what you want?" Lucas stood on the other side of the stone handrail of her stoop, facing her. He rested his elbows on it, studying her.

She tried to read his expression, but she got distracted by the sight of his finger-tousled dark hair and the memories of her hand sifting through the strands.

"It was a mistake," she answered belatedly, her throat a little dry at the direction of her thoughts. "One we should get under control before we... head to Miami."

It would be hard to leave her mom, all the more so after the news of her fall. But she wanted to root out this spy for Lucas. Helping him find the guilty party would ease her conscience about not telling him she'd been approached for information on Deschamps.

The high-end beauty conference offered a good opportunity to find Lucas's spy and assure her own name wouldn't come up as a potential traitor.

Lucas nodded slowly, seeming to consider her words. "And how do you suggest we do that, exactly? Get the sexual chemistry under control?"

Just the words revved her up, her body responding automatically. Her nipples perked up. Her thighs pressed against the ache between them. Could he see her reaction?

At the moment, she wished the street outside her building was busier if only to distract her from the temptation of his presence. But except for a neighbor's speakers blaring jazz a few doors down, the night remained quiet.

"Willpower?" she suggested, her body so sensitive that even her hair blowing lightly along her shoulders felt sensual. "Determination?"

"I'll tell you the truth, Blair. Before we kissed, I was barely getting through days on willpower to stay away from you." He reached over the stone handrail to lift a strand of hair away from her cheek and settle it on her shoulder. "Now that I've tasted you? Now that I know you want me, too? It's going to be a battle to keep my hands to myself."

Oh, no.

Blair felt certain that if the stone partition weren't between them, she would have glued herself to him all over again to take up where they'd left off on the rooftop.

"I might be in over my head." Her voice sounded so tremulous, so lost in desire, she forced herself to straighten where she stood. To insert a few inches between them. Because she *had* to be strong. She couldn't afford to go down this path with him, no matter how tempting. "But, damn it, I need this job, Lucas."

"Blair—"

"I mean it. I can't risk letting a personal attraction thwart the biggest opportunity of my professional career. For that matter, I can't jeopardize my spot in this building, either. I could never afford to live in New York otherwise."

Lucas straightened, too, the streetlamp nearby casting his face in shadow as he stepped back from her.

"In that case, we'd better find a way to maintain our boundaries," he conceded, sounding more resolute than she felt. "I need your help to root out a potential spy. I don't want you to be uncomfortable around me because of what happened."

She wouldn't call it uncomfortable precisely. But she wasn't going to quibble when he'd agreed to back off. That's what she'd wanted, after all.

Even if the distance between them, and the new chill in the air, left her feeling empty. Lonely. And more than a little curious about what it would have been like to meet him under other circumstances, where they could have pursued the attraction. She didn't have a lot of experience with men, not with her life being dominated by her mom's health concerns the last year. But even based on what little she knew, she felt one-hundred-percent certain that being with Lucas would be off the charts incredible.

"Thank you," she murmured finally, well aware her plan to cool things down wouldn't have worked without his aid. "And thank you for offering to drive

me to see my mom tonight. I feel okay about waiting to see her until the morning, but it was really
kind of you."

Lucas shoved his hands in his pockets, scuffing a
toe along the pavement. "I can't imagine how stress-
ful it must be to have her far from you when she's not
well. I'm close with my mother, too, as you've probably guessed. I can understand dropping everything
to go be with her when she needs you."

Her heart tugged at his words. His empathy.

"You're sort of doing that for your mom now by
working with Deschamps Cosmetics, aren't you?
Leaving your own business to make sure hers suc-
ceeds." She admired that. Wished she could be half
as helpful to her mom through her cancer struggle.

She shivered. Hugged her arms around herself.

"I'd do anything to assist her." Lucas's gaze was
steady on hers, the magnetic pull between them so
strong she might have swayed toward him in spite
of herself. The moment lingered. Potent and full of
possibility. But then he stepped back. "You'd better
head inside, Blair. It's cooling off out here."

In more ways than one.

Swallowing the guilt and anxiety, Blair wished
him a good night before retreating indoors, away
from the draw of a man she could never touch again.

Five

"Honey, you should leave now if you want to make your train," Blair's mom told her late the next afternoon.

Weakened by the powerful drugs she received to battle her cancer, Amber Westcott had slept most of the day in a living-room recliner at the rented Catskills cabin. After arriving late that morning, Blair had made a big batch of chicken noodle soup, painted her mother's toenails and tackled some cleaning. For the last hour, she'd worked on a jigsaw puzzle that was a picture of a cheesy heartthrob from an old television show her mom liked. Her mother had been too tired to help, dozing on and off.

So it pained Blair a tiny bit that her mom made it a point to remind her it was time to leave *twice* in the last five minutes. It almost made a daughter feel unwanted, despite her best efforts to be helpful. Her mother was the one suffering, after all. She had every right to be alone if she preferred. Blair couldn't help it that *she* really needed these visits to reassure herself her mom was okay. And she tried not to hover or be a nuisance. Oddly, she found herself wishing she'd confided more in Lucas the night before. She couldn't help thinking he'd understand.

Now, seated on a wooden footstool near her mom's recliner, Blair straightened the pile of magazines on a weathered pine coffee table to put them within easy reach. Then she studied her mom, taking in the white bandage peeking out from the pink-and-green cotton scarf tied around her head. She'd lost her hair three weeks ago, but she seemed to have made peace with that, claiming she appreciated a streamlined grooming routine while exhausted, anyhow. She'd lost about ten pounds in the last month, her thin frame angular-looking under the gray throw blanket that covered her from waist to feet. Pink house slippers stuck out from the blanket.

"Mom, I found a shortcut back to the train station, remember?" Blair's cab driver had taken a long way out of the mountains the first time she'd visited the cabin, making her think the trip took longer than it should have. "My Uber won't be here for a few more minutes. Are you sure you're okay where you fell yesterday? You don't need me to rebandage your knee before I go?"

The cut on her mom's knee had been a surprise finding. Valerie had mentioned that Blair's mom had hit her head when she'd phoned the night before, but not the second, bigger gash on her mother's knee that had a vivid black-and-blue mark around it today.

"I definitely don't," her mother retorted, mustering enough spirit to kick aside her lap blanket and bare her leg, a teasing light in her blue eyes. "But I know you won't let it rest until you see for yourself."

"Sorry to hover." Blair *did* feel better to note the bandage appeared clean and dry. She straightened the soft gray cashmere again, not meeting her mother's eye. "A few more minutes and I'll be out of your hair for a whole week."

"You're not in my hair. I don't have any, remember?" Her mother yanked off the headscarf and tossed it aside with an exasperated sigh.

Empathy pinched. "Oh. Mom. I'm—"

"Don't." Her mother squeezed her hand where it rested on the arm of the leather recliner. "Don't say you're sorry anymore. I know I'm cranky, Blair, and I don't mean to take it out on you when you mean well. But sometimes you're just so damned careful around me—"

She stopped herself, biting her lip and turning

away to fiddle with one of the pieces of the forgotten jigsaw puzzle on the folding card table near her chair.

"Careful?" Blair prompted, confused but wanting to know what was on her mother's mind since she hadn't said much today. "You mean like gentle? Shouldn't I be careful around you when your body is going through so much?"

Her mother slammed down the puzzle pieces, causing a few to jump. "I mean you treat me like I'm old and infirm. Like I might break from a cut on my knee."

She sounded so annoyed. So frustrated. And Blair knew she shouldn't take it personally. But Blair felt a little battered today, too. She hadn't slept well after the way she and Lucas had parted. Especially when she knew she'd have to see him again. Work with him again. Travel with him to Miami. Knowing all the while he was every bit as tempted by her as she was by him. According to him, he'd been drawn to her even before the kiss.

It hurt to think that he'd confessed as much when she hadn't been completely honest with him. Part of her still wondered what might have happened if she'd simply come clean about her former employer's efforts to learn more about Deschamps Cosmetics. So yeah. She wasn't at her best today, either, because she was doing everything she could to help her mom, and it felt like her mother only wanted her gone.

"I don't mean to be overly cautious. But I think

it's only natural to worry about someone going through…everything you are."

"Cancer," her mother snapped, frustration evident now as she balled up the headscarf in her hand and squeezed it in a tight fist. "You can say the word, Blair. I know I have cancer. You don't have to dance around it."

Blair swallowed. Her eyes burned to see her strong mother, the woman who'd coached her field hockey team and could run and shoot and pass as well as any girl on the team, red-eyed and angry, hurting with a pain Blair couldn't help her bear.

Outside the cabin, the shadow of a vehicle in the driveway told Blair her ride had arrived.

"I'll do my best, Mom." Rising from the footstool, she kissed her mother's forehead. "You're stronger than me, though. You look cancer in the eye the same way you've stared down every obstacle in your life." Divorce, financial hardship, working two jobs when times were toughest. "When I dance around it, I do it for me. Not you."

Heading toward the cabin door, Blair picked up her bag to take her leave. She glanced back at her mom as she opened the door, wishing they were parting on a happier note.

But her mother only laid out the headscarf on her lap, smoothing away the wrinkles from where she'd wadded it up. Suppressing a sigh, Blair regretted frustrating the person she loved most in the world.

Next visit, she would need to take a page from her mother's book and be stronger. Tougher. Confront things head-on without ducking from the thorny bits.

Maybe the sticky situation she found herself in with Lucas would be a testing ground to become a more formidable version of herself. Or, more likely, she'd just made the world's most transparent attempt at justifying her need to see him even though she knew they'd be better off remaining far, far apart.

Just over a week had passed since the rooftop kiss with Blair before Lucas saw her again.

She sat two seats over from him in one of the smaller conference rooms at Deschamps Cosmetics for a meeting to finalize plans for the upcoming beauty conference. The marketing director was still reviewing the strategy for a new product launch, but Lucas's thoughts kept straying to Blair. Even though she wasn't in his direct line of sight, she still dominated his peripheral vision. In front of her was the empty tin that had contained her homemade lemon-frosted sugar cookies at the beginning of the meeting. There wasn't even a crumb left inside it. He knew because he'd arrived too late to sample one, but everyone had raved about them.

Now, he was aware of her every time she typed a note on her tablet. Her pale pink fingernails tapped lightly over the screen in a way that made a braided string bracelet slide free from the sleeve of her cream silk blouse.

A humble and incongruous accessory for a woman who, like many in the competitive beauty industry, dressed with creative flair. Today's outfit, along with the simple ivory blouse, included a pair of brown leather walking shorts and a gold necklace threaded through the belt loops instead of a belt. His interest in fashion was nonexistent, but his interest in Blair had him lingering on the sight of her. His thoughts were interrupted when the head of marketing suddenly called Lucas out.

"—so unless Lucas has anything else for us, we can wrap the meeting?"

Was there a worse way to hand someone the floor than that? Now, eight people were ready to sprint for the exit while Lucas did, in fact, have something to add. He rose to his feet, wishing his gaze didn't move to Blair first and foremost.

She eyed him, too, however, the color in her cheeks heightening a shade at his regard. That couldn't be by design, could it? He felt sure her re-action to him was real enough, no matter whether she had deeper designs on Deschamps Cosmetics than she let on.

"Just one thing," Lucas began, shifting focus to address the gathered staff who would leave for the beauty conference in Miami in two days. "A reminder that what we've discussed in here about the soft launch of Deschamps's new antipollution makeup line is one-hundred-percent privileged. Even after the products go live at the conference, we keep the marketing direction strictly under wraps."

He emphasized the point by planting both palms on the conference table, leaning in to meet the eyes of each person seated around the sleek expanse of polished oak.

The marketing director looked uneasy as she shuffled a few papers from her presentation into a manila folder. "Of course that's true. I would hope the staff is well aware—"

"I wouldn't expect you to give reminders every time we bring up confidential information," Lucas offered, giving her an out. But had she looked uncomfortable because she felt chastised by his remark? Or could there be any hint of guilt there? He'd been so focused on Blair because she was new to the company. "Yet this company is at an industry crossroads, and there are parties who would be very interested in what we're doing. I simply thought it a good time to remind everyone the stakes are high, and we trust your commitment to Deschamps."

The room remained silent in spite of it being the end of the workday. For a few uncomfortable moments, everyone seemed to forget their rush to leave. It was no secret the beauty industry, worth over five hundred billion a year, could be cutthroat.

Lucas used that quiet window of time to study

the group again. When his gaze reached Blair, she looked down at her wrist, using one finger to trace the links of the braided string bracelet he'd noticed before. Frustrated he hadn't started on her side of the table, he regretted not seeing her immediate reaction to his words.

The marketing director, he'd noticed, looked him directly in the eye. The difference between one woman's demeanor and the other's was unmistakable. Although, taken alone, hardly an indication of guilt. Still…

A recent random review of company-wide browser visits and email exchanges had flagged a few potential problem contacts on Blair's device. Nothing concrete, of course. Visits to competing sites and conversations with industry contacts were natural. And normally, welcome. But the threat of secrets leaking had him on edge.

"Thanks everyone," he said finally, straightening to dismiss the meeting. "That's all for today."

Lucas withdrew his phone while the group exited the conference room, then scrolled through his inbox for updates from his own business. He'd been away from his office for weeks, plus the distraction was necessary at a time when he struggled to keep his eyes and thoughts off of Blair.

A moment later, however, after the room went quiet, her voice called to him from the exit.

"Lucas?"

He stopped midscroll, barely reading anything

on his device, anyhow. Glancing up, he took in the way she'd stalled at the threshold, one hand on the doorknob, the other clutching the empty cookie tin. She wasn't looking at him, though. Her attention seemed fixed on the floor for a long moment after she'd said his name.

"Yes?" Everything in him went on alert, his whole body attuned to this woman no matter how many times he'd told himself he couldn't trust her. Needed to stay away from her.

When she lifted pale blue-green eyes to his, she appeared troubled.

"In the meeting, you mentioned the company is at a crossroads," she began slowly, releasing the handle of the door so that it closed behind her. Leaving the two of them alone in the conference room. "And that the stakes were high for Deschamps with other companies wanting to know what we're doing."

He tensed. Shoved his phone in his jacket pocket while he considered how to answer. Was she fishing for details because she was the leak? Or because she knew something that might lead him to the right person?

"That's correct." He took a step closer to her, caught himself and halted again while they remained a few feet apart.

Memories of her lips against his robbed him of sleep on a nightly basis. Memories of the sounds she'd made while his hand crept up her thigh were imprinted in his brain to replay again and again. How could he think of anything else when he stood this close to her?

"Can you tell me why?" She ran an idle finger along the edge of the bright red cookie tin, tracing the rolled edge of the lid.

"Certainly. I assumed everyone in this room was aware that Deschamps has been struggling for the last few years. We've received a generous buyout offer from a larger beauty conglomerate, and several of the board members want to accept."

"But you don't?" She arched an eyebrow at him. Curious.

He hoped it wasn't an act. Hell, it unnerved him how much he wanted her to be the thoughtful baker of cookies, the compassionate caretaker of a sick mother and a committed makeup artist. Not a corporate spy. He ground his teeth in frustration.

"What I want is immaterial. This is Mom's company. She built it from scratch and fought to make it a success. So if she doesn't wish to sell, that's all that matters." He understood Cybil Deschamps's attachment to the business went deep. The company's success had helped her save face when the extent of her husband's philandering went public. He gave her a lot of credit for channeling her hurt into something positive.

Blair nodded, her fingernail tapping a thoughtful rhythm against the tin she carried. "I understand that. And yet, I can't help but think you seem…personally offended at the idea of someone buying out Deschamps."

Did she honestly not know?

Lucas speared a hand through his hair and turned from her, trying to weigh and measure his complicated feelings for this woman. Damn, if he knew the best way to answer her when half the time he suspected her, and the other half of the time he wanted to kiss her again.

"My father's company, DLH Luxe International, is the potential buyer," he answered, giving up trying to figure out her motive for the conversation. At least for the moment.

Besides, it wasn't like the news was secret. If she didn't hear it from him, she'd certainly learn the truth of the matter in Miami. He leaned back against a credenza by one wall, settling in for the conversation in a way that kept some distance between him and this too-tempting woman.

"*He's* the one who wants to buy out Cybil?" She sounded so indignant, Lucas almost smiled. "Doesn't that seem—" She shook her head as she seemed to struggle for the right word, strands of her blond hair dancing with the movement. "Mean? He must know she's not interested in selling."

She set aside the tablet she'd been carrying and placed the empty tin beside it. She took a seat to half lean, half sit on the oak credenza near him, bringing the sight of her killer legs with her.

Lucas dragged his gaze up to her face, but the warm vanilla scent of her only teased his nostrils and made him hungry for a taste of her.

"You must not have read enough tabloid stories about your landlord when you won the spot in the brownstone," he observed dryly, gripping the edge of the oak cabinet on either side of him. "A cursory search of my mother's name yields endless results about her tumultuous relationship with my dad and the acrimonious divorce during my senior year of high school."

His father had made their lives as difficult as possible, manipulating friends and family members alike into thinking the worst of his soon-to-be ex-wife. And, of course, he'd had the kind of wealth that kept the divorce settlement tied up in court for years.

"I had no idea," Blair said softly, tracing a design on the Persian carpet with the toe of her taupe-colored leather sandal. "This year has been so surreal for me with my mother's—" She went still, her toe halting on the carpet. Then, after letting out a long breath, she continued. "Cancer. She has ovarian cancer."

Her words changed the trajectory of the conversation, throwing everything that came before in shadow as this new development came to light.

He didn't think twice about touching her. His arm was around her a moment later. Squeezing. Hugging. Comforting. And, feeling how she sank into him, leaning against him, ensured he'd never regret it. Whatever else was at work between them, this was real. Painful.

"I'm so sorry." His lips found the top of her head. Kissed her there. "I understood she was ill, but I didn't realize it was that serious."

He would have held her longer, but she straightened then and rose from the spot on the credenza. She paced away from him while she spoke.

"I hadn't shared it with anyone else until recently. But last weekend she helped me see that I need to confront the reality of what she's facing. Stop hiding from the diagnosis in fear, and look cancer in the eye."

Lucas reshuffled all the things he knew about Blair, seeing her in a new light. The sunny, optimistic disposition that he'd read as hiding something. The nonstop baked goods that he'd viewed as a way to win over people she wanted information from.

Regret filled him as he realized she'd been trying to keep her own fears for her mother at bay.

"That can't be easy to do, Blair. It's only natural to be fearful when someone you love is in a fight for her health." He hated that he'd thought the worst of her.

Protectiveness for her surged, mingling with the guilt, making him want to pull her against him. But, damn it, she'd wanted some distance between them. She'd asked him for that. So the best thing he could do now would be to honor her request, even when it went against everything he wanted.

Maybe she'd change her mind in Miami. At least now, they'd be working together to find the mole inside the company instead of him having to be suspicious of her all the time. That was a relief.

Blair paced toward him again, then gathered her things off the conference table. "I know. It's just been such an intense few weeks that sometimes I don't know up from down, let alone all the elements of corporate drama at Deschamps Cosmetics."

When she offered him a wobbly attempt at a smile, he recognized that she needed to change the subject.

She'd shared enough regarding a topic that made her uneasy.

"Maybe the trip to Miami will be a good thing for you." His heart thudded harder against his chest, reminding him how much he wanted her. Needed to hold her and taste her again. "I'll bet you could use a getaway."

A delicate wash of pink flooded her cheeks. He would have given his left arm to know what she was thinking just then.

But she only nodded. "Maybe so."

Then, just when the awareness between them started to simmer again, she backed away from him and hurried out the conference-room door.

He let her go. For now. But now that one barrier between them had been eliminated, he wouldn't hesitate to pursue her when the time was right.

Six

Alone in the back seat of a large, chauffeured SUV two days later, Blair crumpled a medical bill in her hand as the vehicle descended into the Holland Tunnel on the way to Teterboro Airport. Her whole life felt like a descent lately, with her mother's healthcare expenses mounting, her dwindling savings and her fears for her primary position given the way Lucas hunted for a spy within Deschamps Cosmetics.

She couldn't afford the latest bill, which made it imperative she find additional work ASAP. The proceeds from selling her mother's house had gone toward the surgery bill and had paid for the cabin rental. But when her contact from her old firm,

About Face, phoned her again this afternoon, she'd let loose a tirade about her refusal to provide competitive intelligence on Deschamps Cosmetics. So it had taken her by surprise when she finished her rant that her former company actually wanted her to freelance a commercial makeup job for an editorial photo shoot. And the pay was really good.

She'd verbally agreed to the extra work, even though it made her a little queasy to accept anything from the company that had tried to make her spy on Deschamps. Not to mention, she'd been reeling a bit since learning that About Face had surely been tapped to coordinate the spying mission by management at a higher level, since the company was one of many owned by the powerful beauty conglomerate that Lucas's estranged father headed. Knowing the elder Deschamps wanted to take over Cybil's company made the move seem all the more treacherous.

But at least Lucas was well aware of his dad's machinations. Any guilt Blair felt about not sharing her interactions with About Face was minimized by the fact that Lucas recognized where the threat originated. She had every intention of helping him find his spy.

After tucking the bill away into an outer compartment of her leather handbag, Blair spent the rest of the afternoon in the rush-hour drive to the airport, and took the opportunity to formally accept the freelance makeup job in a text. Knowing she would have that added income eased some of the stress that came with the bill weighing down her purse like her own private albatross.

Hitting Send as the driver pulled into the airport drive, Blair stowed her phone in her bag in time to see Lucas waiting in front of the terminal building. He'd texted her earlier in the day to let her know the details for the private flight that would take them to Miami, adding that they would have dinner on the plane. The rest of her colleagues had traveled early that morning on a commercial airliner. But as Lucas Deschamps's personal guest, Blair would experience the conference in an entirely different way.

Her nerves stretched and tightened at the thought of how much they would be on the road together this weekend. So it made no rational sense that a little part of her was thrilled to see him waiting for her on the tarmac, dressed in a charcoal-gray suit, a pair of dark aviator sunglasses hiding his eyes as he beat the chauffer to open her door.

"Hello, Blair." He offered his hand to help her from the vehicle, the warmth of his fingers stealing her breath as they wrapped around hers. "You look beautiful."

She missed a step as she processed the compliment, the words sounding more intimate than their usual exchanges. She still hadn't gotten used to the fact that they didn't bait one another anymore, their interactions forever changed by the night on her rooftop.

"Oh. Um. Thank you." She glanced down at her white halter-neck dress with a handkerchief hem, a pair of heeled red sandals completing the outfit. Then, her eyes darted to him as he signaled to an attendant, indicating an aircraft visible behind the terminal for one of the airport's fixed-base operators. "I wasn't sure of the evening's schedule, so I hope this is appropriate."

She'd changed three times, in fact, nervous about traveling with him and what it meant that she'd agreed to this. He wasn't her direct boss, but as the man who would inherit the company, there was definitely an employer-employee relationship at work.

"There is no schedule." He returned his attention to her, his hand shifting to the small of her back as he guided her forward lightly. "This trip is going to be a break for you. You've been working too hard."

Keeping pace with him, she heard the baggage cart rolling along the sidewalk behind them, an attendant minding the practical details of travel so that Blair had no choice but to focus on the man beside her.

"Even so, I don't intend to slack off on this trip. I hope you'll outline your expectations about my responsibilities—" Blair halted, both her words and her step, as she spotted a catering truck backed up to the private jet in front of them. The van had the name of an exclusive lower Manhattan French restaurant emblazoned on the side.

The restaurant wasn't notable simply for its celebrity chef and impossible-to-secure reservations. Blair had heard the food was outstanding.

"What's wrong?" Lucas paused, as well, apparently feeling her hesitation.

Even the rumbling wheels of the rolling cart full of luggage stopped.

"Is that our plane?" she asked, glancing around the runways, curious why a meal from an ultraexclusive restaurant would be part of their flight.

Lucas's lips twitched. "Where else would I be taking you?"

"Oh. When you said we could eat on the flight, I guess I envisioned prepackaged sandwiches and a bag of nuts." She continued walking, reevaluating the trip and what it meant in terms of her relationship with Lucas. The gesture—if she was interpreting it correctly—seemed to be setting a romantic precedent. Then again, maybe he simply liked eating well. "I even baked raspberry tarts. You know, just in case the alternative was packaged cookies that were broken and crumbling before you even opened them."

She was rambling, obviously. But her nervousness had ratcheted higher. Perhaps Lucas sensed it, because his palm flattened on her back, allowing her to feel more of the warmth and weight of his touch. He bent to speak close to her ear.

"I only wanted to do something nice for you. My sole expectation is for you to relax over the next few days. Finding the spy is secondary." His words triggered a shiver down her neck and all the way down her spine.

A shiver he must have felt where his fingers rested on the small of her back.

But he released her then as they reached the red carpet at the base of the jet's narrow stairs. Standing aside, he gestured for her to proceed ahead of him. His thoughtfulness, his careful solicitude of her feelings since he'd learned of her mother's illness, only added to the attraction she'd been fighting since they met.

By now, the catering van was pulling away from the small jet, although a uniformed waitstaff member remained close to the runway. Lucas greeted the man while Blair headed up the metal steps and into the opulent world of the *über*wealthy who could afford things like private planes and personalized catering from the best restaurants in Manhattan. As her eyes adjusted to the dimmer interior lighting of the cabin, she took in the leather seating—four facing forward, and two facing one another in the back, plus a couch that sat parallel to the aisle. An open door in the rear of the plane showed a fresh floral bouquet near the sink of a lavatory.

A little dazzled that this would be her ride to Miami, Blair's finger trailed over the embossed silver plate that read Bombardier Challenger 350. The scent of lemon polish mingled with hints of something savory beneath silver-domed dishes filling the counter in a prep area for refreshments. But no matter how impressive this display might be, she couldn't help but think the amount of money spent on this trip alone would surely cover the bill in her purse.

She was still taking it all in when Lucas joined her, a hint of summer breeze behind him.

"Let's take a seat back here so Rawdon can begin the service before we take off." As he indicated the seats facing one another in the back, Lucas unbuttoned his jacket.

Her gaze flicked downward to the movement that drew her eye. Oh, who was she kidding? It was the lean frame beneath the jacket that caught her attention. His crisp white dress shirt disappeared into the gray trousers at a point that called to her hand.

Luckily, she felt the plane rock slightly beneath her feet, as their bags were stowed in an exterior luggage compartment, the motion snapping her from her reverie. Her face warmed as she hurried down the aisle where Lucas had pointed, then dropped into the nearest leather seat. Carefully, she set her oversize shoulder bag by her feet since it contained the tarts she'd baked.

While she smoothed the hem of her dress over her knee, she reminded herself she should *not* be ogling him. And she definitely didn't deserve this royal treatment.

Especially when she hadn't been forthright with him. But she would fix that by helping him find his spy.

Dragging in a long breath, she tried to relax and just get through this. And maybe, just maybe, she'd find a way to enjoy a little bit of the journey the way Lucas had suggested. Surely she could focus on the upcoming meal without getting distracted by the even more delectable man?

She flicked up her gaze in time to see Lucas slide strong arms out of his suit jacket before laying the gray silk fabric on the sofa across from their seats. Then, he folded back his shirtsleeves, revealing forearms that were just flat-out sexy. Muscles flexed in them while he worked, smoothing and tucking the white cotton with military precision before he leaned forward to hit a button between their seats and release a sleek fold-out table so that an eating area appeared.

Only then did he take the seat across from her, his golden-brown eyes locking on hers and somehow making all her nerve endings tingle at the same time.

Dinner from the five-star restaurant hadn't even started, and Blair already knew the man across from her would be the most tempting thing at the table.

Looking back over the course of his dating history, Lucas couldn't recall ever making a woman nervous before. And he sure as hell hadn't meant to with Blair, but he could have sworn that was the vibe he was getting from her when they'd first arrived at his jet.

Thankfully, somewhere between the appetizer course of oysters and the main course of duck breast with field cherries and endive, he sensed her relax a fraction. The bottle of Lafite Rothschild Bourdeaux may have helped, but Lucas couldn't help hoping he'd put her at ease, as well.

"Are we ready for raspberry tarts?" he asked Blair as they finished their main course.

Their server cleared the dishes for them before tactfully disappearing into the prep station at the front of the aircraft.

"And deprive ourselves of whatever mouthwatering confection is hidden under silver domes up front? I think not." Smiling, she leaned back in her seat and refolded the white linen napkin over her lap. "Everything we've eaten tonight has been amazing."

"I'm glad you've enjoyed it." Seeing her savor the dishes had been even better than the food itself, as far as he was concerned. Ever since learning about the stress in her life with her mother's illness, he'd made Blair's pleasure a point of emphasis for this trip. "And I won't keep you from whatever Rawdon brings out next. But since I've never tried your baking, and it is the talk of the office—"

"You haven't?" Frowning, she leaned down to retrieve her bag from alongside her seat. "I assumed

I must have fed everyone in the company ten times over by now."

"I'm always too late," he said, dodging the topic, not wanting to admit he hadn't sought out her wares because he'd been convinced she used the baking tactic to ensure none of her colleagues thought she was a mole. "Although I nearly scored a German chocolate cupcake last week. But Mina, my mother's assistant, spotted the pastry at the same time as me, and she got a scary look in her eye that made me think she'd bite my hand off it I took it."

Blair laughed as she placed the bag on her lap, rummaging through it for a moment before withdrawing a clear container. "To be fair, those are her favorite."

While she returned her bag to the floor, their server arrived with a plate of bite-size profiteroles for them to share, along with a bottle of sparkling rose to pair with the dessert. Rawdon popped the cork, then poured them each a glass before departing.

Lucas glanced meaningfully at the carton of tarts that Blair still hadn't opened. "I hope you're not going to deny me my first chance to sample something you've baked."

She shook her head, blond hair skimming her bared shoulders in the halter-necked dress she wore. He'd be seeing her in that dress when he closed his eyes tonight.

"Certainly not." After prying up the lid on one

corner of the small receptacle, she slid it across the table toward him. "Just keep in mind that while my baked goods are delicious compared to the candy bars in the lobby snack machine, they're definitely not in the same league as the work of a professional French pastry chef. Okay?"

"Duly noted." He had to fold back a layer of wax paper to reveal four round pastries with scalloped edges, filled with what looked like vanilla cream or custard, topped with raspberries and lightly dusted with sugar. "Wow. They look like works of art."

"That's not the real test, though," she warned him, reaching for one of the chocolate-covered profiteroles on the silver serving tray between them.

She took a tentative bite of her dessert, the sound of pleasure she made reaching right over the table like a stroke over his fly. He ground his teeth together to keep his jaw from dropping at the sexy exhibition she hadn't intended.

Damn.

Hunger for her stirred and stretched, unwilling to be ignored. For a long moment, he breathed through the need to sweep aside the remnants of the meal and take her on the table. Because that would be the wrong approach, even though the image persisted. When he finally dragged his thoughts back to their dessert, he tore into the tart with more force than necessary, knocking loose a couple of berries as he did.

Between the light, flaky crust, the mild sweetness of the fruit and the rich vanilla bean flavor of the custard, the dessert was incredible.

"No wonder the whole office swoons at your feet on baking day." He locked eyes with her, knowing that as good as the tart tasted, she would taste even better. "This is fantastic."

"Thank you. But are you swooning?" She arched a playful eyebrow at him, and he was grateful to see this side of her.

Then again, maybe it had always been there for everyone else to see. He'd just been so caught up in thinking the worst of her he hadn't been able to get a genuine read on her character.

He polished off the tart and helped himself to another.

"To be honest, I was closer to swooning when I heard the sound you made after you took the first bite of yours." Nodding toward the plate of profiteroles, he had the satisfaction of seeing her color rise.

Awareness darkened her gaze to aquamarine. Even as she glanced away from him and returned her attention to her dessert.

"Having spent many days baking, I can't help it that a perfect pastry is a source of personal bliss."

He wanted to pursue a line of questioning about other potential sources of personal bliss for her, but he could see she was flustered, and he wasn't ready to press the obvious attraction.

Yet.

"Where did you learn to bake?" he asked instead, wanting to use this time to learn more about her.

They were scheduled to touch down in Miami soon. And while his main goal for the trip was to give her some time to relax, he also planned to get to know her much, much better.

"My mother is an exceptional cook." Finishing her second puff pastry, she patted along her lips with the linen napkin before taking a sip from her water glass. Something about the deliberate way she moved made him think she needed to steel herself to talk about her ailing parent. "Mom studied briefly under a pastry chef before she had me."

"That's impressive." He hoped she would keep speaking, certain that her mother's illness was behind some of Blair's reticence with him.

"She hoped to open her own restaurant one day." Enthusiasm for that plan shone in her eyes for a moment before dimming again. "But over time that dream faded. Raising a family required more time and income than an apprenticeship afforded, especially once my father left."

Her withering tone conveyed a lot about where her dad ranked in her affections. Before Lucas could reply, their server returned to clear the dessert dishes and prepare for their descent.

Once Rawdon disappeared to the front of the cabin to pack up the food service, Lucas continued.

"Your mother must be proud of how well you picked up her skills. It has to be rewarding for a parent to see their offspring succeed at something they're passionate about." He wished there wasn't a table between them so he could be closer to her, but perhaps having the barrier there would help him stay focused on getting to know her.

Blair shrugged half-heartedly, appearing unconvinced as she leaned back in her seat.

"I'm not sure. I went a long time without even touching a mixing bowl since we were living in places with really limited kitchens." Her gaze darted to his and away again. "Baking can be an expensive pastime between the ingredients and the necessary tools. So I've only just rediscovered how much I enjoy it since being in the brownstone. The kitchen is a cook's dream."

"I guess that would have never occurred to me," he said slowly, acknowledging the blind spot of his economic privilege. "I would have thought as long as there was an oven, you'd be all set."

"An oven definitely helps," she said wryly, her shoulders straightening a fraction. "Back when I was in grade school, Mom rented a place that came with a hot plate and a refrigerator."

That visual helped his understanding of her past come into sharper view. But seeing the way defensiveness sparked off her, he needed to be careful how he acknowledged it.

"Fair warning—your colleagues at Deschamps will likely revolt if you move back into a place with a hot plate." Although he'd make certain that didn't happen.

Blair's talents deserved to shine.

She rewarded him with a laugh, making him feel better than…

Hell. He couldn't recall the last time he'd felt as good as the way that laughter made him feel. The way *she* made him feel.

Seeing how Blair's momentary happiness all but turned him inside out, Lucas felt the first prickle of warning about what pursuing her might mean. He couldn't afford the distraction of a relationship right now when his mother's business was on the brink and he had his own professional responsibilities to return to. He wasn't even staying at Deschamps Cosmetics after the threat of the buyout disappeared. Besides that, he'd grown up with a front-row seat to how quickly a relationship could turn from unhappy to downright toxic.

Long before his parents' marriage had finally dissolved, Lucas had decided that keeping things simple with the women in his life would be better for everyone.

So no matter that he might feel attracted to Blair beyond the physical, he would concentrate on the payoff of taking her to his bed. There, they could indulge in the way that would be most rewarding for them both.

Tonight, he'd keep things low-key. Give her a chance to settle into the expansive two-bedroom suite he'd booked for them to put her at ease. But tomorrow, he'd commence his plan to enjoy their time together fully. A weekend of pleasure and then they'd move on.

And if the moments when she laughed occasionally caused his chest to tighten with something deeper? He'd damn well learn to ignore it.

Seven

Rumor has it the new Deschamps antipollutant line will be amazing! You should bring a sample to the shoot.

Blair stared at the message on her phone the morning after her arrival in Miami's famed South Beach. It had been part of an innocuous exchange with a former coworker at About Face. Destiny was a makeup artist she'd been close with at her old job, and she looked forward to working with her on the commercial photo shoot that Blair had signed on for next week. They'd chatted briefly about the booking before Destiny mentioned the new product line. And, of course, she wanted a sample. In the beauty business, everyone lived for samples.

Why, then, did Blair go cold at the request? Destiny was her friend. She wouldn't be trying to score advance access to the chemical components in the proprietary formula to give Deschamps's competition an advantage, would she?

Gripping the phone tighter as she sat at the rosewood dressing table in her private bathroom of the two-bedroom suite she shared with Lucas, Blair willed away the surging panic. She was being paranoid now.

Of course, she wouldn't share a sample from the new skin-care line containing powerful pollutant screens. Now that she'd become invested in helping Lucas find the company leak, she was simply seeing nefarious schemes everywhere.

Blair set the phone on the dressing table, then slid it away. She couldn't think about this now. Not when she needed to leave the Setai, a luxurious South Beach hotel, to make the short walk to Miami Beach Convention Center and do her job. Despite all the stressors heaped on her shoulders lately, she couldn't help looking forward to the beauty conference and the escape from real life that it represented for a few days. She'd gotten into the business because she loved it, but sometimes she forgot how much in the push to make the work as profitable as possible for her mom's sake.

Selecting a chunky lip pencil from the curated travel bag of her personal makeup favorites, Blair smoothed on the matte formula in deep rose, the finishing touch to her face. She didn't normally wear much makeup to work, but at a beauty conference, the bar was set high. Both vendors and visitors would showcase their best looks, and if she was tapped to spend time greeting guests at the Deschamps Cosmetics display, she needed to represent the brand.

She stood back to eye herself critically in the ebony-framed full-length mirror outside the dressing area of the master suite that Lucas had insisted she take. The Asian-inspired decor in the minimalist hotel was soothing, and the understated browns and creams only set off the jewel-tone blues of the Atlantic Ocean outside the windows. The neutral furnishings made her bright pink cloque-fabric dress stand out, too. The fitted sheathe dress with high neck and generous cutouts down the front and back was a long-ago thrift-store find with a designer label she could have never otherwise have afforded. These days, even her thrift-store budget was nonexistent.

Blair picked up her purse from the king-size bed and stepped out into the common area of the two-bedroom suite. Lucas had plans for the morning to take care of some personal business in downtown Miami, and he had encouraged her to sleep in after their evening flight.

So her steps faltered when she spied him on the

outdoor terrace, a newspaper folded on the café table beside him as he took a call. What was it about the sight of him in his ivory dress shirt and black pants that made her pulse race?

She hesitated in the kitchen area, laying her clutch on the breakfast bar, the scent of coffee lingering in the air. He must have returned from his morning meeting while she'd been showering, since she'd never heard him. And why did she have to think about being naked at a time when her heart already thumped like it would leap right out of the cutout down the front of her dress?

The dynamic between them had shifted radically over the last week, making her nostalgic for the time when Lucas had barely spoken to her. She could deal with brooding, judgmental Lucas. It was charming, thoughtful Lucas that threw her off her game. He made her feel, at turns, guilty for not coming clean in regard to the overtures About Face had made toward her, or else desperate for his hands on her. The whiplash of feelings made her wish she'd slipped out of the suite before he returned.

Eyeing him through the French doors to the terrace, Blair was about to make a dash for it when Lucas pocketed his phone and stepped into the kitchen.

Sultry sea air followed him inside. But it wasn't the warmth of the outdoors that made the room feel suddenly too small.

It was *him*.

He stopped just inches from where she stood, his gaze roaming over her as if he hadn't seen her for weeks instead of hours. Or was she projecting how she felt? Because she mentally measured the span of his hand where he rested it on the granite countertop, thinking about how it would feel running up her thigh. And she may have lingered a little over the sight of his mouth, recalling how it fitted to hers so perfectly. Her fingers itched to smooth along his jaw to feel the texture of skin there. The hungry perusal stirred awareness, heating her skin in a slow wave.

Calling up desire she couldn't act on.

"I was just getting ready to head to the convention center," she blurted in a breathless rush. "To work," she added with a bit too much emphasis.

Beside her hip, his hand flexed where it was lying on the countertop, one knuckle rapping lightly against the granite. Otherwise, the kitchen was so quiet she could only hear their mingled rapid breathing.

Though her heartbeat pumped so insistently, Lucas might be able to hear that, too.

"I thought I made it clear you should take some downtime?" His dark eyebrows swooped down, drawing together as he contemplated her.

"I did." She needed to devise boundaries. Fast. "I already slept in, which was something I haven't done in ages. But now I'm ready to mingle with the rest of the Deschamps employees to see what I can learn about your spy."

She needed to find the traitor in the company. The shadow of guilt about what she hadn't told him ensured she'd work twice as hard to find the leak.

He seemed to weigh her words for a moment. Considering.

Finally, he nodded. "I'll go with you."

Relief flooded through her, along with a tiny, unreasonable hint of disappointment that they couldn't act on the attraction. But before she could reply, Lucas lowered his head to continue speaking. More quietly, this time.

"Tell me one thing first. Before we go."

The words brushed over her skin like a caress. Her nerve endings danced. She made herself stand very still, even as his scent enticed her closer.

She could only nod in response, her throat too dry to speak. She was so tightly wound she was practically vibrating as she waited for him to say something.

But first, his fingers grazed her cheek, a light touch that tipped her face up to his. For one breathless moment, they took each other's measure.

Then, his thumb trailed lower, settling beneath her jaw in a soft, vulnerable place where he had to feel her heart race. When he spoke again, his voice was deep and silky, calibrated to turn her inside out.

"Do you ever think about that kiss we shared?"

* * *

Lucas promised himself he'd let her go soon.

He refused to use the attraction to his advantage, needing her to make the next move. She worked for his mother's company, after all. And she'd already admitted that she couldn't afford to compromise her place in the brownstone. Lucas knew his mother would never hold their relationship against Blair when making decisions about her employment or a coveted spot in the prestigious Brooklyn women's residence. But he wouldn't give Blair more reasons to feel anxious when she was already dealing with an ailing parent.

All he could do was line up this opportunity for them to be together. Give her the chance to act on the chemistry if she so desired.

He wouldn't use his touch as coercion. This brush of fingers along her pretty face hardly counted, right? But he'd be damned if he'd pretend the attraction didn't exist.

"I think about it sometimes," she admitted softly, her breath a teasing caress against his knuckles as she spoke.

He wanted to feel her breath on his lips. Taste her words on his tongue. Seal her body to his.

"Not enough to want a repeat, though." He muttered the thought aloud as his thumb outlined her jaw. Chin to ear. Back again.

"Enough to know if I kiss you again, all I'll want

is repeats." She met his gaze, her eyes darkening so that just a thin rim of pale green was visible.

Her words stirred hope for the weekend even as she kept that damn boundary in place. He stared at her, mesmerized by the way she seemed to sway closer without ever touching him. He could have their clothes off in seconds. Hell, he didn't even need her clothes off in that dress she was wearing.

"You'll let me know if you need a refresher." His thumb sketched along the plump fullness of her lower lip. Pressed slightly when he reached the soft center. "If you'd like to reevaluate."

He breathed in the vanilla scent of her, a fragrance made more complex by the warmth of her skin.

Her mouth moved beneath his touch. "Do you honestly think we'd get to the conference if I take you up on that offer?"

The possibilities inherent in those provocative words fired over his senses while his personal Blair Westcott wish list scrolled through his mind's eye. And damn, but he wanted to lick his way through the berry color she wore on her mouth to taste beneath it. No cosmetic could enhance the natural beauty of the woman.

"So make it a condition." He wasn't letting go of the option she'd left on the table. "You hold all the cards, Blair. Insist that I get you to the conference in exchange for one kiss."

He'd give her that and a whole lot more. If he

only knew precisely when this woman had become so important to him—but he couldn't question the intensity of what she stirred inside him.

He couldn't even think straight when she was around, and there was only one cure for that. Only one way to quiet this heated fascination.

"Fine." Her hand circled his wrist, holding him in place as he cupped her face. "I'll count on you to make sure I walk out of this room in five minutes."

He couldn't miss the challenge in her tone. The flash of excitement in her eyes, or the way her fingers pressed into his forearm. All those signs of her hunger fueled his. Reminded him that he wasn't in this haze of desire alone.

Blair felt it, too.

"And?" He dropped his forehead to hers, his heart slamming against his ribs. "In the interest of making sure we're on the same page, what do you want to happen in those five minutes? A kiss?"

He needed to be clear. Needed her to be sure after the walls she'd carefully erected around herself.

But when she closed the distance between them, leaning into him with her delectable body, he realized he needn't have worried about that. The press of her curves sent a very definite message even before she spoke.

"I want you to make me forget everything but you, Lucas." Her hips rolled against his. "Please."

Hell.

Of all the ways she enticed him, it was the *please* that turned the last of his restraint to ashes.

Gripping her hips, he lifted her against him, her body gliding over his easily thanks to the silky dress she wore. He backed her against the refrigerator, pinning her between his body and stainless steel, holding her steady for his kiss. Once they were eye-to-eye, her quick breaths warming his lips, he gave her mouth an experimental lick.

She tasted like a destination. Like heaven. Like somewhere he'd never want to leave.

Her body went slack against his, sighing into him, giving way to his touch. That subtle relinquishing of power, handing herself over to him, was a turn-on like nothing else. Having earned this moment with her, he'd cut off his own arm before he gave her any reason to regret it.

So no matter that his body was on fire to be inside her, he focused all his attention on her mouth. He sucked on the full lower lip, pulling it in his mouth to sample. Her flavor imprinted itself on his brain, minty, sweet and uniquely her. He needed more of her, so he released her lip to twine his tongue around hers.

Her whimper smoked along his senses, making his hips press harder into hers. But he couldn't think about how good that felt, or he'd never tear himself away. And this wasn't about him. Blair needed something from him, and he would provide it. He wanted to be the one she came to for this. For what she needed.

He wanted to be the *only* one.

The ferocity of the possessiveness was foreign to him. But he didn't question it because Blair wasn't like anyone else. The effect she had on him was exclusive to her alone.

He broke for air, gratified to see her eyes were still closed. Her lashes fluttered slowly before they opened, her expression as passion-dazed as he felt. Her lipstick was gone, the natural color of her swollen lips taunting him with how much more he wanted from her.

For now, this had to be enough.

"I can make you forget everything else all day long," he promised, stroking his fingers through her silky blond hair. "All you have to do is say the word."

Her focus returned slowly, but she nodded.

"I believe you could," she mused aloud.

"You deserve that escape." He didn't release her yet, not ready to sacrifice the feel of her against him.

Her pale green-blue eyes tracked his, a wary shadow passing through them.

"You don't know that, Lucas." A sigh huffed from her lips, her tone sounding strangely defeated. "How could you know what I deserve?"

Understanding the moment had passed, even if he wasn't quite sure why, he lowered her to the floor at the same time he backed up a step. His body protested the loss of her immediately, and he had to ball his hands into fists to keep from pulling her back to him.

"An educated guess," he said simply, hating every breath he took that wasn't scented by her fragrance. Far from easing the need for her, the kiss had only reminded him of how much he wanted this woman. "And you're not going to dissuade me of my opinion."

She didn't answer, but lifted a hand to her hair, smoothing the ruffled locks with an abrupt gesture. When she did, the simple braided string bracelet slipped out from where she'd hidden it behind a thick gold cuff.

Lucas touched it, tracing the colorful woven band with one finger.

"A friendship bracelet?" He was curious about the incongruous detail.

Curious about her.

Besides, he understood she wasn't ready to discuss that kiss and what he hoped it might mean for their weekend together.

"It is." A smile curved her lips as she glanced down at her wrist. "I know it's not exactly in keeping with my outfit, but it's sentimental."

He watched as she spun it around so that a red-and-yellow series of string sat on top of her forearm while the pink-and-turquoise threads shifted to the underside.

"I'm not the fashion police. You should wear what makes you happy."

And whatever makes you smile like that.

Even if it humbled him to recognize that he could kiss her breathless, but he couldn't put that same light in her eyes. The acknowledgement shouldn't sting, damn it.

Blair reached for her handbag and withdrew a lip pencil, carefully reapplying it to her mouth while she peered into a tiny handheld mirror.

"Some of the weekends I visit my mother, I spend time at the treatment center with other patients," she explained as she shaded the Cupid's bow area. "I'll take my makeup kit and do some of their faces for fun."

He waited while she tucked the pencil and the mirror back in her small bag.

She slipped the purse under her arm before she adjusted the gold bangle over the friendship bracelet, hiding her sentimental side under the fashionable trappings of her professional world.

"And about a month ago," she continued, "a pre-teen whose face I'd done brought me the bracelet as a thank-you." Blair hesitated, shifting her feet. "She made one for herself, too, so that we match. They're our cancer-repelling bracelets."

Blair struck a defensive pose like a superhero, her arm braced across her face like a shield.

And while her defenses were in place, she'd just sent a wrecking ball through more of his.

Lucky for him, her commitment to working this weekend ensured they didn't linger in the suite after that. He accompanied her out of the hotel, making small talk about the conference and his ever-present need to find the leak in the company. He understood it couldn't be Blair. No woman who spent her weekends giving free makeup sessions to cancer patients could be selling corporate secrets.

But without the barrier of suspicion to keep him at arm's length from her, he'd need all his resolve to maintain a strictly physical relationship. It almost seemed like an impossible challenge considering all the kind and good things he knew about Blair.

Until the first person he saw as they reached the Miami Beach Convention Center stepped out of a distinctive gray Bentley and reminded him of every reason not to get involved.

Dread pooled in Lucas's gut.

He didn't realize he'd tugged Blair to a stop beside him until she peered at him, a summer breeze blowing a strand of fair hair across her cheek.

"What is it?" She followed his gaze to the tall man dressed in a tan linen suit and gold-rimmed aviators. "Do you know him?"

"Unfortunately, yes." His grip tightened on her elbow until he forced himself to relax. He couldn't avoid this meeting. "It's my father."

Eight

Blair hadn't even recovered from the kiss that knocked her sideways back in the hotel suite. Her lips tingled long afterward. Her body ached for Lucas, and she hadn't come close to forming a game plan for how to handle what should happen between them next.

So she really felt unprepared to face Peter Deschamps, a man Lucas clearly despised. The same man who had surely used his powerful position to get Blair's former employer to ask her to spy on his ex-wife's company.

But the determined set of Lucas's jaw told her they would be confronting him here. Now. Already,

Lucas guided her closer to the beauty conference's red carpet, a spot for journalists to photograph and interview the stars of the business.

"Lucas." The impeccably tailored man turned toward them, startling Blair with his resemblance to his son as he removed sunglasses from his face. The dark hair might be shot through with silver at the temples, the tawny-colored eyes lightly lined and the grooves around his mouth deeper, but from the straight blade of his nose to the width of his shoulders, Peter Deschamps was a mirror image of his son in a few more decades.

"Dad." Lucas paused again a few feet from his father, his hand relocating from her arm to the small of her back. Tension vibrated through him. She would have felt it even if he hadn't been touching her. "This is Blair Westcott. Blair, my father, Peter Deschamps."

"Your name is so familiar, Blair." The tawny eyes glittered with a different light than she'd ever seen in Lucas's. "Have we met before?"

They'd paused just a few steps from the red carpet, inciting interested glances from the waiting camera crews. There wasn't much activity at this time of day, as most of the celebrities arrived later in the schedule for their panels and meet-and-greets. But Peter Deschamps, owner of DLH Luxe International, would be well known to this crowd.

"No, sir, we haven't." She met Peter's extended

hand, certain they'd never crossed paths. She hadn't even realized that Lucas's father was at the helm of the conglomerate that owned About Face while she'd been working there. "It's a pleasure to meet you."

She thought she heard Lucas scoff at those words, but his father took no notice.

"You, too, of course. I don't have the opportunity to meet many of Lucas's girlfriends." The smile he gave was cool. Unkind. The similarities between father and son began to lessen as he spoke. "Although I'm *sure* your name has come across my desk."

He narrowed his eyes at her, as if determined to pinpoint a connection that didn't exist. Would a man in his elevated position be so involved with the spying efforts on his ex's business that he would be aware of who'd been approached to gather information about Deschamps Cosmetics?

Wariness set her on edge. Ahead of them, a photographer lifted a camera, dialing the focus button as she aimed the lens their way. Blair tried to maintain a relaxed expression, mindful of how photos from this event would be circulated widely.

"Blair used to work for one of your companies," Lucas informed his father, his palm steady at the base of her spine. "If you'll excuse us—"

"That's where I know the name." Peter Deschamps smoothed the dark brown floral tie he wore with his tan linen suit. "About Face." He winked at her, as if they shared a secret. "I'm sure I heard about your contributions."

The comment was harmless enough. Flattering, even, if overheard by someone outside their conversation. But to Blair, the way he said it, combined with his smug expression, intimated something else.

Did he think she'd accepted her former employer's proposal that she spy on her new company? The idea shouldn't bother her. She hadn't done any such thing. Yet worry tugged at her.

"Thank you," she murmured belatedly, only nudging out the response as Lucas urged her down the red carpet toward the waiting doors of the venue.

A quick glance over her shoulder at Peter Deschamps showed the older man still watching her, a speculative look in his too-familiar eyes.

"Lucas, give your mother my best," he called after them.

Beside her, Lucas showed no reaction, save the flexing of his jaw.

As awkward as the exchange had felt on her end, her gut told her it had been even more unwelcome for Lucas. She could see no trace of the would-be lover who'd tempted her beyond reason with his kiss less than half an hour ago. In his place was the brooding, cold Lucas she'd known for her first six weeks with Deschamps.

She wanted to ask him about his father, but they were required to pose for photos before entering the building, a task that Lucas silently agreed to and that they performed with surprising ease. How quickly she tucked against him, her hip brushing his thigh, her breast to his chest, while he kept her under one arm.

She smiled on cue, her heart beating fast at the feel of being this close to him while the photographer snapped a few pictures. Something about the way she and Lucas moved together, their bodies seeking one another's, reinforced what their earlier kiss had taught her.

Sooner or later, she would be in his bed.

She'd been so focused on not having a physical relationship with him in order to protect her job, she'd lost sight of the fact that they'd already grown too close to save her from rumors to that very effect. She was in Miami as his guest, and their image together would broadcast a more intimate relationship, anyway. Why should she deny them what they both obviously wanted when their associates probably already assumed they were sleeping together?

"Ready?" Lucas asked her as the photojournalist walked away, leaving them free to enter the beauty convention.

Blair, for her part, remained plastered against him like it was her job. She straightened now, a new resolve putting a different complexion on the weekend.

She would still do everything she could to help Lucas find whoever was responsible for leaking Deschamps Cosmetics secrets. And she hoped she could do so before her upcoming freelance job with About Face so that she didn't need to feel guilty about her continuing association with one of his father's businesses.

But no matter what else she accomplished during her time in Miami, she wasn't backing down from something she wanted for herself, just this once. She would accept Lucas's offer to make her forget everything else. With all the stress of the last weeks weighing on her shoulders, she craved the escape she could find in his arms.

At least for the weekend, until the real world came calling again.

"How's it going in Miami?" His mother's voice sounded through Lucas's cell phone.

He'd just returned to the convention center five hours after leaving Blair there to network and enjoy the conference. It hadn't sounded like a fun way to spend an entire workday to him, but she'd insisted on taking the mission seriously to find the leak in their organization. Besides, she was more connected to the industry than him, and seemed genuinely excited to check out the full scope of the event.

For his part, he hadn't wanted to spend any extra time under the same roof as his father, even if the Miami venue boasted five hundred thousand square feet of exhibit space. So Lucas had left to check in with a few local clients of his own. Now, walking through the jam-packed hall full of social media stars doing meet-and-greets with fans, visitors taking photos in elaborately designed selfie sets and reps from major beauty houses demonstrating new products on excited guests, Lucas had to step toward the slightly quieter perimeter to take his mother's call.

"I only just arrived on site," he explained while a throng of security guards bustled past with a music-industry VIP in the middle. A trail of determined fans with raised cell phones followed in their wake. "So I'm not sure what kind of response we're getting to the displays yet."

"I've already spoken to Blair, and it sounds like the new product line video is eliciting a lot of interest at the booth," his mother returned. Normally, she enjoyed attending beauty conferences like this one, but she was still working on plans for the roll-out of the new product now that they'd moved up the launch of the antipollutant line. "I'm more interested in the run-in you had with your father."

"Blair told you about that?" His grip tightened on the phone at the memory of his dad's behavior toward Blair.

Peter Deschamps hadn't been overtly rude, but something about his cagey manner seemed calculated to make her feel uneasy. Almost as if his father had been hinting that he'd heard something negative about her job performance. It definitely got Lucas's hackles up, as if just talking to the underhanded bastard wasn't bad enough on its own.

"She didn't have to tell me, darling. There are photos of the three of you all over social media." The sound of a keyboard tapping preceded a notification chime on his end. "I've just sent you a couple of links."

He hastened his progress toward the Deschamps Cosmetics exhibit, anxious to see Blair in case there'd been any fallout from meeting his dad. "Any reason I need to see them? I thought it was a reasonably civil interaction."

Sidestepping a giant prize wheel for a game to win all types of eyelash extensions, Lucas spotted the green-and-white logo of his mother's company hanging from the high ceiling a few rows away.

"Was it?" his mom asked dryly. "You'd never know that from your expression in the pictures, Lucas. You're glaring daggers at him. Although there are other photos of just you with Blair that are…" She paused a moment, as if thinking how to best express herself. "Well, suffice it to say you look happier in them."

Curious now, he stopped beside a support beam off to one side of the aisle, trying to stay out of people's way while he checked the links his mom had sent him. Sure enough, the image of Blair with his father showed Lucas scowling in the background. A caption read Rumors of the Deschamps Family Rivalry Confirmed.

The social media posts only reinforced what he needed to keep in the front of his mind this weekend. Divorce and broken relationships only led to unhappiness for all parties concerned. That's why he preferred to keep things simple.

"One second, Mom," he said, hoping she could hear him while he scrolled through two similar images with captions—Luxe Dynasty Heir Dethroned? and Tracking the Rift in the DLH Empire.

"I'm just looking at these now. You know I have no intention of accepting a role at DLH—"

He stopped on the picture of him standing beside Blair. He didn't see whatever captions might have appeared with the photo because he couldn't take his eyes off the way they looked together. She leaned into him like she was made to be there. Seeing her hand on his chest, her head tipped toward his shoulder, reminded him exactly how she'd felt against him. She stared into the camera while Lucas stared down at her, his expression…intense.

Sort of like he wanted to devour her whole. Which shouldn't be a surprise since that's exactly how he felt around her. He just hadn't realized it radiated off him stronger than a strobe light.

The thing that *did* surprise him? Something in Blair's expression told him he wasn't alone in that feeling. She seemed fully on board with testing out the chemistry between them now.

"Hey, Mom. Hold that thought." He brought the cell phone back to his ear as he charged through the conference-goers toward the Deschamps Cosmetics booth. "I've got to go. Thanks for sending these."

Disconnecting, he felt a moment's regret that he hadn't filled her in on the encounter with his dad, but all his thoughts were on finding Blair. He edged around a makeup model dressed like a fairy, purple wings taking up half the aisle, then took a shortcut between booths to reach the only woman he wanted to see.

As he finally neared the display area for his mother's company, however, he stopped short. Blair wielded a cosmetic sponge in front of a bright cabinet full of eye-shadow palettes, a rainbow of color backlighting her as she bent toward a thin, grandmotherly woman dressed in tennis shoes and a threadbare sweater. The older woman laughed while Blair swept the sponge over the well-lined face.

The sight of Blair lavishing time and care over a customer outside the industry's primary demographic didn't surprise him in the least. In fact, now that he was starting to know her better, he would have been more startled to find her applying makeup to a more traditional beauty.

She must have felt his gaze from his position several feet away, because she paused in the act of selecting a mascara and peered behind her. Visitors to the booth passed between them carrying sample bags stuffed full of product giveaways, but Blair's gaze held his.

And he knew then that something had shifted between them since that morning. He felt it in the open way she stared, saw it in the heat simmering in her eyes. As his temperature spiked, his body oblivious to everyone else around them, Blair turned away to finish work on the woman seated in her makeup chair.

Lucas did his best to will away the worst of his need, but he wanted her *now*. Already he was cursing the size of the exhibition hall and how far they'd have to walk before he could be with her somewhere private. At least he could shave off a few minutes by calling for a car to pick them up outside the convention center so they could drive doorstep to doorstep.

And damn, but he hoped he hadn't read her wrong.

While he made the arrangements for the vehicle, Blair looked into a hand mirror with the older woman. She appeared to be explaining how she'd achieved the makeup look, gesturing around the lady's cheeks and temples.

Even to Lucas's untrained eye, he could appreciate the warm glow of her client's face. But was that because of makeup, or pleasure from Blair's consideration? He knew firsthand how good it felt to have her undivided attention.

A moment later, and Blair was by his side, her customer having vanished into the stream of conference attendees. He wanted the right to pull her against him, memories of their earlier kiss plaguing him.

"Are you ready to leave?" he asked without preamble, shoving his phone back in the pocket of his jacket.

He took her hand, uncaring what anyone else thought about the gesture. But then, he hadn't been worried about the security of her position with Deschamps in the first place. Blair had been the one who'd wanted to avoid him. But the photo of them together was already fuel for gossip, so he'd at least enjoy the pleasure of touching her openly. She glanced down to their joined hands briefly, but didn't retract hers.

"I am." Her voice was pitched low, but even with all the noise bouncing around the huge space, he heard her clearly.

"Good." With a nod, he pivoted on his heel and led her to the far side of the convention center, weaving through the crowds.

Behind him, he heard the tapping of her heels as she followed, keeping pace. Minutes later, they were outside in the bright Miami sun, the heat still significant even though the afternoon would soon be evening. The courtesy vehicle from the Setai pulled up to the valet stand at the same time and Lucas led her toward the luxury SUV in the steamy Miami heat.

"We're not walking?" She sounded puzzled, but she continued to go with him. "The hotel is so close."

"Not close enough." He nodded to the driver as the older man opened the back door for them. "I've been thinking about you all day," he confided in her ear as she preceded him into the air-conditioned interior.

"Is that so?" she asked, settling into the leather bench seat and smoothing her skirt around her. "I thought you were working."

"Not well. Not when I had that kiss on my mind every other minute." He withdrew his phone while the driver shut the door behind them. "And once I arrived here, I found this."

Pulling up the image of them together, he flashed the screen in front of her so she could see the picture.

He watched as the color rose in her cheeks. The sight of that pink flush forced him to bite the inside of his cheek to will away the urge to cover her mouth with his right then and there.

"I've seen it," she admitted, lifting her eyes to lock gazes with him. "And so has everyone else working the Deschamps exhibit today."

"I hope that didn't make you uncomfortable." Because while he didn't care what anyone thought of him, he recognized that she'd wanted to keep a lower profile for professional purposes.

The car moved away from the convention center, heading west toward Collins Avenue and the string of oceanfront resorts that lined the beach side of the street.

"Mostly it hampered my efforts to catch the company spy." She tucked a long blond wave behind her ear. "Who is going to confide in a woman who is… so close with the boss?"

"Are you?" He turned more fully toward her, his phone screen going dark as he dropped his hand to her knee.

She bit her lip, teeth sinking into the plush fullness. When she answered, her voice sounded smokier. "Am I what?"

"Close to me?" His heart jackhammered inside his chest. "Are we going to follow through on the attraction this picture suggests we already have?" He waved the phone without turning it back on. "Because I'll be honest, this photo damn near singed my eyebrows off when I saw it."

"Me, too." She nodded slowly while the SUV pulled up to the curb in front of their hotel. "And, yes, I'm ready for that. Um… Ready to follow through," she clarified.

Relief rushed through him even faster than the accompanying sense of victory. Because he didn't know what he would have done if he was still all alone in this need.

"Good." He was out of the vehicle a moment later and helping her to her feet.

The thirty-eight-story building blocked the sun as they stepped onto the sidewalk. A uniformed bell-hop opened a set of double doors for them and Lucas tucked Blair close to his side while they entered.

He picked up his pace to reach an open elevator cabin, all the more motivated by the fact that it was empty. Letting go of her hand to jog the last two steps, Lucas stepped between the closing doors to keep them open. Blair crossed the metal threshold a moment later, and he hit the button to seal them in privacy.

He only needed to hold back for one more minute. Two, tops. Just until the elevator reached their floor, and he got the door to the suite open.

He could wait. Even though the vanilla scent of her skin beckoned, the V between her breasts was visible through a strategic cutout in the front of her dress, and her chest rose and fell so fast he could swear she was fighting the battle for restraint as much as he was.

But the waiting stopped when Blair grabbed the lapels of his jacket in her fists, pulling herself against him. Then, lifting up on her toes, she seized his lips for a kiss that spiraled out of control as soon as it started.

Her lush mouth shredded his restraint. He pressed her against the elevator doors, bracing the back of her head in his palm as he licked into her. The throaty moan she made was the sexiest music he'd ever heard, and he wanted to hear it over and over again. She arched into him, her breasts calling to his hands.

He skimmed his free hand over her body, hip to breast and back, feeling his way around her curves. But it wasn't enough. Not nearly enough.

Reaching lower, he found the hem of her skirt and slid his fingers up the smooth skin of her thigh. It had been so long since he'd touched her this way. Since that night on the rooftop. She made a sweet, purring noise as she lifted her leg to wrap around his hip.

Hell, yes.

He gripped her knee, needing to hold her right there, when the elevator chimed, and the doors slid open behind her.

Nine

Blair would have tumbled right out the elevator doors if Lucas hadn't hauled her around and set her on her feet beside him. Her head was swimming from that kiss, her eyes unable to focus on anything but him. She was so worked up she could be falling out of her dress and she wouldn't even know it.

Vaguely, she felt along the front of the pink fabric and found the cutout between her breasts was still keeping her covered. The gesture drew Lucas's gaze there, and the possessive growl he made thrilled her to her toes. She'd never been an exhibitionist, but if preening a little in front of this man incited that kind of reaction, she wasn't averse.

The elevator doors began to close again, startling her from passion-fogged thoughts. Lucas guided her into the hall and withdrew a room key from his pocket just as they reached the door of their ocean-side rooms.

Her whole body hummed from touching him. And from the knowledge that soon, she would be touching a whole lot more of him.

Finally inside the living area, Lucas let the door shut behind them, then stalked deeper into the room. Blair dropped her purse onto a nearby end table before she followed him, the view of the Atlantic spread out in front of them in a wall of windows as he turned to face her.

She told herself not to jump him. She'd made the first move in the elevator, crushing the lapels of his suit jacket in her rush to get her hands on him. Plus, there'd been that time on the rooftop when she'd demanded he touch her.

Yet now that she'd made up her mind to be with him, she didn't want to waste a second of this time.

"Care to share what you're thinking right now?" he asked as he shrugged off the jacket and laid it over a high-back leather chair around a tree slab table.

"I'm wondering if you can help me set a land speed record for undressing."

He raised an eyebrow before making slow, deliberate work of loosening his tie. She liked watching him as—prompted by her words—he went to work on his shirt buttons with methodical precision.

She also liked the *V* of his chest as more of his body became visible. He was beyond gorgeous, with hard, steely pecs and ridges between delineated abs. Her breath went shallow, her heartbeat racing.

"I could be inside you faster if we didn't undress," he countered, stalking closer as he wrenched off the shirt and let it fall to the table.

"Oh." She gulped air, her eyes snagging on the dark trail of hair that disappeared into his pants. "That is, yes."

His throat worked as he swallowed hard, tawny eyes flashing with heat. And then, he was on her, his hands cupping her ass through her dress and hoisting her up his body. Another moment and he backed her against the door they'd just entered, putting them in the same position they'd been in the elevator.

Only now, they didn't need to stop.

Blair wound her arms around his neck, clinging to him, grateful he understood exactly what she wanted. Needed. His hips thrust into hers, anchoring her, and she groaned at the contact. His lips fused to hers, tongue teasing, seeking, exploring.

She lost track of all the ways he was making her come undone. Everywhere he touched felt incredible. Everywhere he kissed threatened to set her on fire. The press of his erection through her dress, exactly where she needed him, made tension coil inside her and he hadn't even touched her there yet.

Her hips twisted, needing more.

"Lucas," she whispered, breaking the kiss. She wrapped her legs around his waist, wanting him closer. "Please hurry. I've been waiting—"

"You?" He shook his head to disagree, kissing his way down her cheek and grazing his teeth along her jaw. "I've been waiting longer, Blair. I've needed you since that night on the roof."

The ache inside her increased.

"All the more reason to take your fill now." She lowered a hand to smooth over his shoulder, skating along the hard warmth of his chest.

"And I will," he promised, reaching beneath her skirt to palm her thigh. Squeeze. "Just know that that waiting hasn't been easy. You've been killing me. Every." He slid his fingers inside her panties and stroked over her. "Single." Another stroke. "Day."

The last stroke almost sent her over the edge. She was that ready. That close.

She clenched his shoulders, her head falling to the side as pleasure chased through her.

"I thought if we ignored the chemistry it would go away." Being with him was a risk, then and now, but she couldn't pretend the attraction didn't exist. Not anymore.

Lucas's eyes darkened as he slid a finger inside her. "And how did that work out?"

His voice rasped in her ear, the ragged sound making her think his control was slipping as fast as hers. Because she thought she might die if he stopped touching her, her whole world narrowed to this.

Him.

"It only made me think about you more." She kissed her way up his neck, then fisted her fingers in his hair to hold him steady while she met his gaze. "It made me want this even more."

She worked her hips against him, needing pressure. Friction. His chest shuddered in answer.

"Then maybe waiting wasn't such a bad thing." He let go of her, keeping her pinned to the door with his body.

She whimpered at the loss of his touch, but then he unfastened his trousers. She grabbed fistfuls of her skirt, lifting it out of the way, desperate to feel him.

"Can you reach into my back pocket?" He hooked a finger around the scrap of lace that covered her and tore it easily, removing another barrier.

"Gladly." She plunged both hands into his pockets, squeezing the rock-solid muscle beneath and retrieving a condom packet from the left side. She held it up between them. "Can I do the honors?"

"The sooner you're touching me, the better." He planted his hands on either side of her head against the door, his muscles rippling as he leaned closer to kiss her.

She had only a second to appreciate the way he

looked—all ripped, intense male focused one hundred percent on her—but she knew she'd never forget it. He was devouring her so thoroughly it took her a few tries to rip open the foil package, but in the end she unrolled it with shaking hands, easing it over the impressive breadth and length of his straining erection.

Oh.

Anticipation fired through her. He was impossibly hot and hard.

Before she let go, she gave an experimental pump of her hand around him and he imprisoned her wrist so quickly it made her breath catch.

"I'm going to love you touching me later. After this first time." He let go of her wrist as he looked into her eyes. "I need to be in you first."

She nodded fast, like a bobblehead doll, a little rattled by the *L* word cropping up in conversation but fully on board with his plan. "Yes. *Please*, yes."

His hands fell away from the door and reached under her dress to palm her ass. He cupped her, lifting her.

Her pulse went wild.

Then he sank her down on top of him.

The pressure. The fullness. He was everything she'd craved, and more, but the suddenness of it sent her hurtling against his chest so she could adjust to him.

"Are you with me?" he asked, his chest rising and

falling like he'd been sprinting. He kissed the top of her head through her hair.

Even now, her body relaxed a fraction as she got used to him. She tilted her hips experimentally, and he sucked a breath between his teeth.

"Yes." Pleasure pooled in her belly. "More."

Lucas withdrew a small way, then returned, the move eliciting seductive sensations. She closed her eyes, giving herself over to him completely.

He gripped her thighs, steering her around him as his hips pistoned faster and then slower, finding what she liked best. Blair held on tighter, fingers scrabbling for a hold on his sinewy form.

Her head lolled against the door, but it didn't matter because the way he made her feel was transcendent. Her thighs squeezed his hips, ankles locked at his waist.

When he reached between them to stroke her, she knew she wasn't leaving this night unscathed. This man was going to give her the best sex of her life, and a level of fulfillment no one else would ever match.

"Open your eyes." His voice in her ear called her out of that bolt of anxiety, pulling her back to the moment as he probed her gaze with his. "I want to see what you look like when you find your peak."

Was it the intensity of his expression, the personal nature of the request, or maybe the gravel in his tone that pushed her to the breaking point? Her feminine muscles clenched hard, a wave of pleasure rushing through her hard. Fast.

Repeatedly.

Lucas tensed, and a moment later, he found his own release. His hips drove into her again and again, stretching out her orgasm, so that it went on forever. Afterward, they slumped into one another, breathing hard as a sheen of sweat cooled on their skin. The scent of him—of them—was an aphrodisiac even after the fact.

"You okay, Blair?" Lucas cupped her chin and lifted her face, eyes roaming over her with a mixture of concern and heat.

"Amazing, actually—thanks." She couldn't help the emphatic, hormone-fueled response when her body felt so sated.

"Good." He brushed her hair from her forehead and kissed the spot he'd cleared. "Because that was just to take the edge off."

An hour later, Lucas had just tipped the room-service attendant and finished setting up a spot for dinner on the patio when he heard the shower turn off in the master bathroom.

Picturing Blair naked in the next room made him question his sanity for indulging in something as mundane as eating when he could be tasting her instead.

But after the intense encounter against the door,

he'd thought it wise to feed Blair and give her a little breathing room before making good on his promise that the first time was just to take the edge off. He'd ordered a light dinner for them, changing into sweats and a T-shirt while she showered.

Now, he was pouring their drinks when his phone chimed. Glancing at the screen, he saw the Deschamps Cosmetics marketing director's name. Felicia.

Grinding his teeth at the thought of work intruding on his evening, he took the call, anyhow. He'd set aside his professional life to help save his mom's company, needing to make it up to her for being complicit in his father's lies back when they'd still been a family. He regretted that bitterly, so he wasn't about to let that mission fail, no matter how much he wanted Blair again.

"Deschamps," he answered, shifting the food tray from the rolling cart to a cocktail table on the patio.

"Sorry to bother you after hours, Lucas," she began, her voice a little unsteady. "But I heard from a friend in the IT department that management has been tracking employee browser visits and emails, possibly because of an information leak. Is that true?"

Irritation flared. "You called—after the end of the business day—about a rumor?"

"It's more than that and you know it, or the IT department wouldn't have devoted so many man-hours to the project," she fired back. "How serious is it? Could it compromise the product launch?"

Her obvious worry mollified him minimally. He'd allowed the search for IT data to fall to the back of his mind in his preoccupation with Blair.

"It's not up to me to discuss my mother's business, Felicia. You realize we're at a professional crossroads with the board meeting coming up." He stared out at the Atlantic as lightning flashed across the sky, illuminating the waves kicking up in a storm breeze.

"Which is why I need to know what's going on! Lucas, I've been your mother's friend since you were a teenager. Don't I deserve an answer?" The woman on the other end of the call huffed out a sigh. "For that matter, has it ever occurred to you to ask me if I've seen anything suspicious in the company from my vantage point?"

Frustration grew as he glanced over his shoulder, ready to be with Blair and not think about the marketing director's imposition on an old friendship. In fact, her calling him instead of his mother raised a red flag for him, making him question the status of the friendship.

"Have you seen anything suspicious, Felicia?" he asked in a voice that—he hoped—conveyed how weary he was of this conversation.

"I have, in fact," she snapped, sounding indignant. "But maybe I should have phoned your mother."

"I agree that would be wisest." His finger hov-

ered over the disconnect button even as she continued speaking.

"Because *she* would be interested to know that
her latest hire has taken a moonlighting job with
About Face for next week," Felicia said, dropping
the information casually enough, and having no way
of knowing how the accusation would affect him.
"*Your mother* might care that Blair Westcott is still
happily doing business with a company owned by
the conglomerate trying to buy Cybil out."

Surprise sucker punched him, followed by a fierce
need to deny even the possibility.

Was she?

Not that she couldn't accept outside jobs. But it
did seem strange she hadn't mentioned it. Especially
after meeting his father today. Suspicion darkened
his thoughts even as Blair emerged from the master
suite, dressed in a lightweight yellow robe and white
socks, her hair damp from the shower.

He couldn't reconcile what he was hearing with
what he knew about Blair. And yet, hadn't the
browser-history data implicated her, too? His grip
tightened on the phone.

"Wait. Felicia, are you suggesting—"

The call-ended message flashed on the screen,
lighting up the darkened patio for a moment before
vanishing again.

What the hell did it mean?

His gaze fixed on Blair as she moved toward him,

the tie of her robe cinching her waist and emphasizing her curves in a way that distracted him when he should be trying to figure out if he'd misread her.

"I heard room service leave earlier, so I figured the coast was clear." Blair stepped onto the patio through one of the open glass panel doors. "The temperature really dropped from earlier. It feels nice out."

Her attention moved to the rolling cart, then shifted to the plates he'd set on the cocktail table in front of the wraparound patio sofa.

"There's a storm blowing in. I figured we could watch it while we eat." He needed to talk to her. So why couldn't he quit staring at the expanse of smooth thigh visible beneath the hem of the cotton robe?

He fisted his hands, unsure how to begin.

"Sounds good." She slid into the deep seat cushion and crossed mouthwatering legs just as a breeze picked up. They were sitting on the balcony but the roof overhung their position by several feet, keeping them out of the weather. "I can tell you what I learned today at the conference."

The words gave him pause as he took the seat beside her.

"About what?" He removed the silver covers from three dishes, revealing the cheese-and-charcuterie plate, burrata and an agnolotti in parmesan cream.

When he'd placed the order forty minutes ago, he'd imagined a very different tone for the meal. Like

Blair on his lap while he fed her from his plate. Or whispering in her ear between bites, telling her all the ways he wanted her tonight.

Now, Felicia's words replayed on a loop in his head.

"This looks delicious," Blair murmured, helping herself to a slice of prosciutto and a serving-sized baguette while he ladled out the pasta, filling her plate before his. "And I was too distracted earlier to tell you what I found out about a potential spy."

He stilled in the act of handing her a plate, trying his damnedest to read her while the sound of the waves crashing increased below them. Was it a coincidence that she brought information to him now, right after he'd heard something potentially incriminating about her? Could she be aware that she was suspected of spying?

"What did you discover?" His knee brushed hers as he leaned closer to settle the dish in front of her.

Awareness speared him. He wanted her again. Badly.

But he couldn't allow that to cloud his judgment where his mother's business was concerned.

"Thank you." She smoothed a linen napkin over her lap before picking up a crystal glass of water and taking a sip. "I spoke with Corey, the woman who oversees the beauty closet."

Lucas nodded, familiar with the small store-room full of product samples in the office. Employees could request samples for client meetings and marketing purposes, although most of the samples in the New York office went to beauty editors of magazines.

"And according to Corey, samples of the new product line have gone missing." She picked up her plate to try the pasta, her lovely face illuminated by another bolt of lightning streaking across the sky.

"Impossible. The research-and-development team hasn't released any samples to share with marketing yet. Felicia had been griping about it for weeks." Lucas had heard her complain about it to his mother, imposing on their friendship to appeal directly to the CEO.

Making him wonder all over again why the woman hadn't phoned Cybil this evening instead of him.

"The samples arrived the day before we flew to Miami, but Corey said there was a whole packet with the box describing protocol for sharing." She shifted to face him, tucking her knees to one side while she tried a bite of her dinner. "And that wouldn't even take effect until after the board meeting."

"Sounds plausible. I hadn't heard about it, but then there is a lot that goes on in the company on a day-to-day basis that doesn't involve me." He'd only agreed to get involved in order to ensure his mother could sell more board members on the idea of keeping the company in her hands.

There was a lot of profit potential in the new product line, and Lucas planned to pitch that bottom line to them.

Blair stirred a fork through her cheese sauce before meeting his eyes. "According to Corey, a sample disappeared from the closet overnight. She went into the office before the Miami flight, and there was one vial of the serum missing."

Thunder rumbled, the storm growing closer.

"Could someone in-house have taken it?" He tried to recall everything he knew about the launch timeline for the new products. It had all been heavily scripted because the formula was proprietary. "Maybe to bring to the conference?"

"That's what Corey thought. But no one here brought it."

"Did she report the incident?" He racked his brain trying to come up with who had access to the storage area.

Surely Blair wouldn't. She was too new to the company. But was this episode intended to distract him from the evidence Felicia had given him about Blair?

"She was in the process of filling out the paperwork to report it when I spoke with her." Blair reached toward the table for her bread, passing him a slice, too. "I guess it had taken her most of the day to track down everyone from Deschamps who'd made the trip to see if one of them had taken the sample."

He mulled over that for a moment, weighing what he'd heard from the marketing director versus this new information from Blair. He'd been convinced that Blair's character was too kind, too generous, to stoop to corporate spying.

So why was he doubting her now?

Because of Felicia's accusation? Or was there more to it than that? If Blair was somehow tangled up in keeping secrets that could harm his mom…it would do a whole lot more than make him angry. Given what they'd shared, it would be a betrayal.

The thunder grew louder, the rumbles closer to the flashes of light that made jagged lines in the sky.

And Lucas knew that no matter how much he preferred keeping relationships at arm's length, he had already crossed a line with Blair. Gotten too close. So should he jump the gun, before he had any real evidence, and end things now? Unthinkable. He refused to believe the worst of Blair on hearsay. But maybe it was just as well to remember that he didn't want to drag deeper emotions into what should be an escape for both of them.

For now, then, he'd tuck away the information he'd gathered tonight for further review. He'd keep an eye on the situation and reserve any judgment until he knew more.

The tactic sounded fair, even if a voice in the back of his head berated him for taking the easiest path to being with Blair again. The thought came at the same time the rain broke, pelting the low wall surrounding the patio, the sound reverberating all around them.

Damn, if the deluge didn't feel like a judgment on his decision-making. But he didn't stand a chance of walking away from Blair tonight.

Ten

There meal finished, Blair padded toward the edge of the terrace in her socks, stopping just before the darkened area on the tile floor, where the summer shower had reached.

She wrapped her arms around herself while Lucas rolled the food cart into the hallway for removal. The breeze was warm, making the occasional wayward raindrop on her face feel refreshing. Watching the storm roll in had been beautiful, and she could still hear the churning of the Atlantic Ocean that had been so placid that same morning.

She'd grown up in Long Island, but nowhere near the water. The life she'd led there seemed a million miles away now, back when she and her mother had both filled their days with work to get ahead, the calendar passing in a happy, busy scramble. It hurt to think how much time they'd invested to achieve their dreams, only to realize how little the material things mattered.

But she wouldn't think about it now, when she had committed herself to taking this short breather with Lucas to enjoy herself. It wasn't selfish for a caregiver to replenish the well now and then, right? She needed her energy for the taxing days ahead. The moonlighting job. The search for still more income. At this moment, Blair only wished her mom could enjoy what she was seeing. The view of the Atlantic here was breathtaking, even at night, thanks to the ambient light and a hazy moon.

"You're still out here?" Lucas asked, stepping out onto the patio after returning.

Broad shoulders outlined by the glow from inside the suite, he looked as appealing in thin gray sweats and a black T-shirt as he did in the more formal attire he normally wore for work. More, maybe, because she felt privileged to see a side of Lucas that not many people were able to view. He strode toward her now and she couldn't suppress a shiver at the thought of him touching her again.

They hadn't spoken about the way the earth moved when she'd been in his arms and backed up against the door to the suite. Had he felt it, too?

"I'm enjoying the storm." Turning away from him, she tipped up her face to feel the rain-tinged air on her cheeks. "After the struggles of the last few months, this feels sort of cathartic."

She felt his warm presence as he drew closer to her side. Glancing over at him, she followed his gaze to the roiling waves.

"How's your mother doing?" He palmed the middle of her back, rubbing a comforting circle through the cotton robe and the sleep T-shirt she'd thrown on after her shower.

His touch made the question easier to answer, somehow. She'd forgotten that aspect of a relationship, probably because it had been so long since she'd been involved with anyone. But the caresses of empathy could be every bit as powerful as sizzling chemistry. She fought the urge to lean into him fully.

She'd lowered enough defenses this weekend. It would be a mistake to return to New York smitten with her boss when her mother's health had to be her priority. Besides, how would she find time to date anyone once she was working two jobs, a reality she needed to face to pay the medical bills? One freelance gig from About Face couldn't provide enough to pay for this month's chemo.

"She's okay. I texted her at lunchtime today and she said she was tired, but her friend Valerie was going to bring her supper. I'm sure that will help."

Blair's shoulder brushed his, making her realize she'd edged nearer to him in spite of herself.

"Good. How do you feel when you're this far away from her?" Lucas's fingers sifted through the ends of her ponytail while the rainfall slowed. "Is it more difficult than normal?"

"Even when I'm in Brooklyn, it's hard for me not to see her with my own eyes every day. I've tried to get her to do video calls, but she hates them. She doesn't like anyone to see her when she believes she doesn't look her best." Blair wished her mother didn't view her as someone she needed to dress up for, but she understood the feeling.

"That has to be a challenge for you." His hand moved higher up her shoulders to the back of her neck, massaging lightly.

She swayed a little on her feet, appreciating the contact. And, yes, the chance to talk about something that preyed on her mind night and day.

"That's why I started bringing my cosmetics kit with me on the days my mom needs to go to the infusion center," she explained. "I would do her makeup to cheer her up, and soon other patients were asking me about clean products that were safe for sensitive skin or requesting that I 'work my magic' on them, too."

Total strangers had gravitated toward her when they saw her reconstructing eyebrows for her mom, who'd lost her facial hair along with the hair on her head.

"You tapped in to a need," he observed lightly,

his gaze still focused on the water, which made the conversation easier, somehow. "That was kind of you to share your talents with them."

"I would be there every day if I could," she told him honestly, feeling the pinch of conscience that she wasn't even in the same state as her mother right now. "But I need the paycheck—"

She stopped herself as she realized how she sounded.

"Of course, I love my job—" she amended.

He turned toward her, interrupting before she could finish.

"Any devoted offspring would want to be by a parent's side to support them, Blair. Of course, you wish you could be with her more." His hands cupped her shoulders, pulling her closer.

How good that felt.

Was it so bad that she wanted to lose herself in him all over again? That she *needed* that escape? Maybe it was wrong to focus on the physical. But the personal connection threatened to overwhelm her when her emotions were already so close to the surface.

"One day, I want to start a business making beauty treatments easier to access for oncology patients," she confided, eager to divert the attention from her issues with her mom. Or her issues with her finances. Her belly tightened with guilt at the way she'd danced around discussing About Face or her upcoming job there. "Maybe bring the services to them at home as they recover so they feel better about going out or having friends visit."

His fingers stilled in her hair before falling away completely. "You should approach my mother about that," he suggested, his tone turning grim. "*After* the board meeting, of course."

Something in his expression darkened, a shadow passing through his eyes. She would blame it on a trick of the weather, but the storm seemed to have quieted. Even the waves were gentler in the wake of the rain.

"Sure," she answered, curious what he was thinking to cause that dark look. But then, maybe thoughts of the board meeting were difficult enough. She knew there was a lot at stake for Deschamps Cosmetics in the upcoming weeks. "Maybe I will."

In deference to his more somber mood, she stuffed aside her business idea. The concept could only be explored in a far-off future, anyhow. She didn't have the start-up capital for something like that when every penny she made was needed to pay bills.

When he didn't speak, Blair's senses buzzed, warning her something felt "off."

"Are you worried about the board meeting?" she asked, lifting her palms to his chest and stroking lightly. "I thought you were in a good position to ward off a buyout now that the new product line is set."

Half his face remained in shadow and half was illuminated from the lights in the living area of their suite. Still, she could see his jaw flex.

"We will be. Assuming no one undercuts our efforts." The sharpness in his tone made her glad she wasn't his business adversary.

"I'm sure Corey's already reported the missing formula to management." She shifted her weight on her sock-clad feet, feeling nervous even though she had no reason to be.

"Will that deter the guilty party, though?" He closed the distance between them, his eyes still locked on hers as he cradled her face in his palms. "That's the question."

Her brain tried to chase his meaning, but it wasn't easy when his nearness brought all that male strength and heat within touching distance. She breathed in the scent of his laundry and aftershave, the soap and smoky notes drawing her nearer still.

"Lucas. It's not easy to answer the question," she protested breathlessly, her fingers skimming over his shoulders. "You must know my problem-solving skills are seriously impaired when we're this close."

Her toes bumped into his. And even *that* was sexy. She couldn't wait to crawl all over him. Taste him. Stroke him.

"Good. I've spent so long waiting to get a reaction from you that it's gratifying as hell to know you get wound up around me." One hand fell to the tie that held her robe closed. He tucked a finger into the knot and freed it, the lapels falling open to reveal her pink sleep shorts and matching T-shirt.

"Well. I'm reacting now." Her hips thrust closer to his, but his eyes zeroed in on her breasts.

"I can see that." He traced the outline of one distended nipple through the cotton shirt.

Ribbons of pleasure fluttered through her as he ran his finger over the pebbled tip, then lowered his head to close his mouth around it right through her T-shirt.

"Oh," she gasped, spine arching toward him as her head fell back. "That feels…"

He drew on it forcefully, making speech impossible. She scrabbled for a hold on his shoulders to anchor herself as her world tilted sideways. Never had anyone made her feel the way he could, like she'd come right out of her skin if she didn't have more of him. Like she'd never feel this much pleasure again with anyone else.

She sank her fingers into his dark hair, ready to keep him there. But he broke the kiss before she secured a good hold.

"We need to find a bed this time. Come with me." He wrapped her hand in his and hauled her inside, closing the sliding doors behind afterward.

She followed him into the room he'd used the night before where a bank of windows had its own door out to the terrace. Lucas hit a button to close the blinds as they entered, then touched a bedside lamp to put it on a low setting. But she only noticed those things in her periphery vision, since her main focus stuck on the white duvet and pillows that seemed to float, cloudlike, over the teak floor. The minimalist design of the room put all the emphasis on that king-size bed.

Then again, maybe the prominence was in her mind and had everything to do with how much she wanted Lucas in it.

He couldn't wait another second to touch her.

Blair hadn't turned around yet, her attention fixed on the bed. So he wrapped his arms about her waist from behind, pulling her back against him. Breathing in her vanilla scent, he buried his nose in her neck, needing to forget about that phone call from Felicia. Unwilling to let unsubstantiated claims ruin his time with Blair.

"I can't get enough of you." He roamed his hands around her belly and hips, feeling her softness through the thin sleep shorts and T-shirt. "Fair warning, but I may keep you in this bed all day tomorrow."

He felt the shiver that ran through her at his words, and damn, but he liked that. Liked knowing he could wind her up.

"I'd settle for staying in it all night," she countered, swiveling her hips against his erection.

Heat streaked through him and he sucked in a breath.

It would be so easy to lift the hem of her robe and touch her this way. Bend her over and ride out the pleasure until they were both panting and spent. Except how long before he wanted her again? And again? He couldn't foresee a moment's peace from thinking about her.

"That's a deal, beautiful." He spun her around to face him in the faint glow from the bedside lamp. "But I need to see you. I didn't get you naked the first time, and that's something I'm going to correct now."

He ran his fingers through the long ponytail, where her hair had dried in waves, then he flipped it behind her shoulder so it wouldn't cover any of what he unveiled.

Her fingers hooked in the drawstring of his sweats, pulling herself closer. But, as good as her touch felt, he untwined her hand so he could slide her robe down her arms and off.

Thanks to the way the bedside lamp illuminated her, Lucas could see the shape of her breasts beneath her shirt. He traced each slope through the material before gathering the T-shirt in his fists and dragging the garment up and over her head.

"Perfect." He cupped the weight of one breast in his hand, lifting it toward his mouth to receive his kiss.

She made a soft sob of pleasure that only revved

him higher, her fingers fisting in his hair to hold him there.

Not that he had any intention of leaving those perfect breasts. He licked and sucked, dividing his attention equally between the swollen peaks. Blair shifted her legs restlessly, letting him know how much she liked what he was doing to her.

"Lucas, please." Her fingers moved to his shoulders, biting into him to get his attention.

Releasing one damp nipple, he straightened to meet her eyes. He recognized the hungry look he spied there. He'd seen it that night on the rooftop in Brooklyn. And again, earlier, when he'd backed her against the door.

She wanted more. Needed more.

And it was all his pleasure to give that to her. Hell, it pleased him just to know he'd put that look there in the first place.

"I'm going to take care of you now, Blair." He stripped off her shorts, intending to make good on his word.

The sultry picture she made warranted at least a moment to capture the way she looked. He'd want to return to this image in his head over and over.

But when she fumbled with his drawstring, her knuckles nudging him through his sweats, he knew he couldn't wait any longer.

Peeling off his shirt and sweats, he watched the

way she eyed him, her lips parting slightly as her gaze dipped south.

Lingered.

His cock strained closer. And a moment later she was on her knees in front of him, spiking his temperature about a million more degrees. The first, tentative strokes of her tongue had his hands clenching at his sides. When she lowered her head a moment later, taking more of him, it took every scrap of his restraint not to hold her there.

He struggled to hold back as she set up a rhythm, working him over with her hand and her lips, driving him higher until he was hanging by a thread.

He mastered himself long enough to pull her to her feet.

"I want to finish inside you," he reminded her, running his hands over her hips and steering her toward the mattress. "And we still haven't made it to this bed."

"Beds are overrated." She kissed him hard, reminding him how much passion lay behind her sweet exterior.

Damn, but she fired him up.

He boosted her up before planting her in the middle of the white duvet. She landed with a little squeak of surprise, her face flushed and her breasts bouncing from the landing.

"You say that now, but you might appreciate a soft landing for your spine when I'm covering you in another minute." He opened the drawer of the nightstand, where he'd stashed condoms.

"That sounds promising." A wicked light in her pale eyes made him want to tease her more to put that expression there again.

His life before her seemed colorless after the heat and passion she'd breathed into it.

Now, he ripped open the package and rolled the condom in place, needing a relief that only she could offer. Wanting to give her that release, too.

Her eyes glazed over as he neared the bed, then levered himself above her. She shifted her legs, making room for him between them, and his heart slugged harder in his chest.

She was the sexiest sight he'd never seen, but Lucas didn't think that accounted for why he wanted her more than he'd ever wanted any woman. It was something unique to her.

Or was it that he had feelings for her?

Shutting down that wildly distracting thought, he focused on the one thing he could control right now. Giving her pleasure.

Poised above her, he eased inside her slick heat. Her body gripped him so tightly, he had to go slowly. Her nails scored his arms, a welcome sting to balance the incredible sensation of Blair all around him.

She lifted her legs to wrap around his waist, taking him deeper. He withdrew, only to return again.

Her breath caught as he sank into her harder, so he did it again.

Again.

He watched as her eyelashes fluttered closed, her cheeks flushing darker. Her moans grew more urgent, and her hips worked to meet his thrusts.

Her breathing shifted to a new rhythm, fast and shallow, and he knew she was close to release. He pressed one of her thighs wider, making room to stroke her sex before he trapped her clit between his knuckles, squeezing.

She flew apart a moment later, her cry filling the room as her feminine muscles pulsed wildly around him.

The sensation was too much. A rough groan wrenched up his throat when his own release slammed through him. The spasms rocked the base of his spine as he gave up everything he had to her.

Long moments later, he hauled in deep breaths, trying to regain equilibrium. Or even just open his eyes.

With an effort, he rolled to one side of Blair, yanking a corner of the duvet over them as he did.

Silence stretched, the air conditioner clicking on to blow a stream over them while their bodies cooled. By the time he rolled over on his side to look at her, she was dragging the hair tie from her ponytail and combing fingers through strands made unruly by their coupling.

He didn't know why the intimacy of that act seemed even more personal than sharing their bodies, but his chest expanded as he watched her. When she caught him staring, a smile flickered over her face and he felt an answering tug beneath his ribs.

He knew in that moment he didn't want this weekend to be the end of their time together. And yet, he couldn't ignore what Felicia had told him. He needed to review the data from the IT department about Blair's browser history and email contacts with her former employer.

Possibly confront her about it.

The knowledge darkened his mood at a time when he only wanted to pull her against him. But he would have shoved it aside again if his phone hadn't chimed just then.

Her eyes darted to his, and he held back a sigh of frustration.

"Sorry, but I should get that." He stretched over her and stepped off the bed to find his phone in his discarded pants pocket. "It's my mom's ringtone."

"Of course." She burrowed deeper under the duvet. "Take all the time you need."

Lucas grabbed a pair of shorts from his bag as he connected the call. "Hi, Mom. Everything okay?"

"The very opposite of okay. It's all fallen apart," she rasped on an anguished note, her voice almost unrecognizable.

His gut sank. He hated hearing the torment in his

mother's voice. She'd already been hurt so much by life—by his dad. What the hell had the old man done now? He stopped on the threshold to the living area, feet turning to lead.

"What's wrong? What's happened?" Ice chilled his veins as he waited.

"Your father has the formula for the new product," she wailed, sniffling. "Deschamps Cosmetics is finished."

The words took his knees out. He dropped to sit on the chair beside a built-in desk.

All their hard work for nothing?

"Impossible. Dad's probably just blowing smoke—"

"He sent me the chemical formula. He *has* it," she continued, voice rising. "If I don't sell to him, he threatened to rush his own version to market. The board will force me to take the deal and sell to him."

No.

Everything inside him rebelled at the thought. His father had already cheated his mom enough, and Lucas had let it happen. He would not stand by and let history repeat itself now. Not if there was anything he could do to save the company Cybil Deschamps had built single-handedly.

"How did he get the formula? Did he tell you?" A dark suspicion pooled in his stomach as Lucas's gaze turned to Blair.

She was sitting up in bed now, fingers clutching the blanket around her shoulders, her face pale. All

Lucas could see in his mind's eye was his father's peculiar attitude and expression when he'd met Blair. There'd been an underlying smugness in his face. As if he and Blair shared a secret.

What if they really did?

"He said he got a sample. I didn't ask him how." His mother's tone sounded impatient, as if the question had no bearing. "Lucas, what are we going to do?"

Cold fury balled inside him, but he needed to control it. Harness it. Figure out his next steps.

And it all started with confronting the woman who'd had the most contact with one of his father's companies in the last six weeks.

"I have some ideas, but I need to get some answers here before we talk through them, okay?" He kept his voice calm. Soothing. He wouldn't let his mother down.

"All right. But can you call me back soon?" She sniffled again, her voice breaking.

"I will, Mom. Don't worry about it." Calm and gentle. That's what he let his voice say.

But he didn't allow his eyes to reflect either of those things as he met Blair's startled green gaze.

When he disconnected the call, he didn't wait for her to ask him what happened. He confronted her the way he should have weeks ago instead of playing games, asking for her help finding a spy.

And all because he'd wanted her.

Regret for his blindness made his voice harsh as he kept his focus on Blair.

"I need to know the truth." His jaw was stiff as he spoke, tension knotting every muscle. "I know you've been in contact with one of my father's subsidiaries for weeks. Did you steal the formula for the new product to give to him?"

Eleven

A noise roared in Blair's ears, like the Atlantic in the storm, drowning out everything else. Except instead of the crashing sea, the rush must have been her blood pressure spiking, or her pulse hammering out of control.

"Ex-excuse me?" She blinked at Lucas, realizing belatedly she was lying in bed naked while he glared daggers at her.

Had she heard him correctly? Because it sounded like he'd just accused her of stealing.

She scrambled to the side of the bed to retrieve her robe, her hand trembling as she lifted the yellow cotton before shrugging into it. She'd feared a confrontation for so long and now it was here…except the accusation was confusing. Her fingers fumbled to belt the robe. She cinched the waist tight, along with the knot, as if the flimsy garment offered any protection from this conversation.

"Did you take that sample, Blair?" His tone was flat, completely devoid of feeling, and unlike any other time he'd ever spoken to her. Even in the earlier days when they'd subtly sniped at one another, there'd been heat beneath it. That had vanished. "Did you pass any other information to DLH Luxe about Deschamps Cosmetics?"

He'd pulled on a T-shirt and shorts at some point. A strange thing to think about when he was accusing her of stealing, maybe. Yet it felt like he'd armored himself for this conversation, too. The generous lover of moments ago was gone.

They faced one another down like adversaries across the bedroom, his spine arrow-straight as he stood by the door, the bed between them like a line drawn in the sand.

"No, Lucas, no. I didn't do either of those things—" Her conscience made her hesitate before she protested more.

"But?" He arched an eyebrow. The muscle in his jaw ticked.

"There is no *but*," she clarified, toes curling against the teak floor. She was certain he'd understand if she explained.

They'd just spent an amazing evening together. Barriers had fallen. She'd given him more than her body, hadn't she? Her heart thrummed wildly, as if to remind her what else she'd given him.

What a daunting time to realize how much of her heart was already in Lucas's hands. But surely that meant he'd listen to her.

He'll believe in you, whispered something wistful inside.

"Then how do you explain all of the emails back and forth between you and your former employer? Which, by the way, is a wholly owned subsidiary of my father's conglomerate." The cold anger in his voice had to mean that DLH Luxe had the sample.

Of course, he was furious. His mother must be devastated.

But did that give him the right to attack her integrity?

Maybe she was reading in to his manner. She couldn't help but remember all the ways he'd been kind to her over the last weeks. He'd offered to drive her to the Catskills that first night he'd found out her parent was ill. He'd given her a prominent role in the *Banner* magazine photo shoot, allowing her to do Cybil's makeup, which would be an important job for her career. Then, he'd insisted she come to Miami as his guest, lobbying for her to take a break from caregiving for her mom.

"I realize that." Taking a deep breath, she knew

the time had come to explain her situation. "I should have told you earlier that I was approached by About Face, but the recruiter I spoke to said our conversations were protected by the nondisclosure agreement I signed during my employment with them."

Lucas folded his arms, looking even more forbidding with his shoulders squared. Had it only been half an hour ago that she'd clutched those shoulders tight and felt the heights of pleasure?

"They can't bind you to them forever. As long as you don't share their industry secrets, they can't prevent you from talking about them."

Regret nipped, but she couldn't change how she'd handled things. "I should have dug out the agreement and read it more carefully to challenge her, but I've been overwhelmed with working as much as possible and taking care of my mother in any free time."

"So you assumed you could continue to plot against my mother and an old NDA would protect your right not to mention it to me?"

Frustration bubbled over. She had tried to grant him leeway—understanding—for the fact that he was clearly upset, and with good reason. Yet the accusatory tone was too much.

"No, Lucas, I did not plot against your mother." She articulated the words precisely so there would be no mistaking them. "I did nothing to violate any standards of ethics in my work at Deschamps."

She had a clear conscience on that score, and it

felt good to fire back at him. Although now that the words were out there, she realized she needed to add a caveat to her statement. She needed to tell him how hard About Face had lobbied for information, even if she hadn't accepted the role.

His lips flattened into a thin line. "Is it true you're working for them next week?"

She reeled back a step, realizing she needed to explain herself. Fast. Attempting to regain her equilibrium, she started again.

"This conversation began in the wrong place." She'd let him run over her with questions instead of simply stating what had happened. "Let me explain—"

"It is true." A great huff of breath heaved from his chest as he straightened. Shook his head. "I can't believe how blind I've been."

"Lucas, listen." She needed to get the words out before any more misunderstandings blew up this conversation further. "I didn't share that About Face had been contacting me because I did nothing wrong. I should have made time to double-check the nondisclosure agreement so I could share with you that they had solicited me to spy for them. And that while I told them no, they might have approached others at your mother's company."

His jaw dropped for a split second, and she saw a hint of pain in his eyes before he masked both reactions.

"You knew this whole time." The words, spoken with a more moderate voice, matched the cooler expression on his face.

"You knew, too," she shot back, more frustrated than ever and, yes, *hurt* that he chose to see the worst in her after everything they'd shared. "You were already aware that there was a spy in your company. You *told* me as much, and I've been trying to help you find out who it is."

Pain sent spiderweb cracks through her chest, the first sign of something breaking. She held still, trying to prepare herself for what was going to happen.

How could things disintegrate so fast?

"Really?" Tawny eyes narrowed at her. "Were you trying to help me pinpoint a spy, Blair? It seems a whole lot more likely that you were just getting close to me to learn more that you could send back to your other employer."

"How can you believe I would steal a formula from *you*, someone I've been…" She struggled to find the right words—words that wouldn't betray the depth of what she was afraid she already felt for him. "Someone I've started to care about? Not to mention, how could you think I would betray your mother that way, when I depend on that spot in the brownstone in order to keep my job and save as much money as possible to pay for my mom's treatment?"

Silence answered her for a moment, the only

sound her harsh breathing in the wake of her passionate rant.

"It won't be possible to keep your spot in the company or in the brownstone after this, Blair. You must realize that." He eliminated her source of income and her home in one easy declaration, cutting her to the core.

"You could really do that?" Her hand flew to her chest, but she knew it wouldn't help stop the damage he'd just inflicted. "You'd be willing to sacrifice *my mother* to strike back at me?"

His expression clouded, a wrinkle forming between his eyebrows as if he wasn't sure what she meant.

Yet that didn't stop him when he retorted softly, "You sacrificed mine, though, didn't you?"

Not in a million years would she have imagined him capable of such cruelty. So it didn't really surprise her when he backed up a step.

"I'm going to make arrangements for a flight to New York within the hour." His voice was cold. Distant. "If you wish to accompany me, you'll probably want to begin packing."

He turned on his heel and already had his phone in his hand as he left the room.

Only then did Blair feel the spiderweb cracks spread the rest of the way around her heart.

Moving on autopilot, because she couldn't afford a plane ticket home without him, she forced herself to pick up her discarded clothes. Then, moving to her bedroom, Blair did exactly what he asked of her for the last time.

She got out her bags and began to pack.

An hour into the flight to New York, Lucas glanced up from his laptop to see Blair rummaging through a gray leather bag at her feet. He sat in the back of the jet, while she'd taken a spot on the opposite side in the front.

He'd barely looked at her since their argument, even though his earlier anger had cooled. He'd poured all of his energy on the trip into gathering information from his mother and reaching out to his father. From the former, he'd obtained screenshots of their communication that he planned to show to the Deschamps board to convince them of his father's lack of integrity and shady business practices. From the latter, he'd received a text that promised a call this evening to "discuss options for the future of Deschamps."

Now, the rustling sound Blair had been making as she looked through her things distracted him from his planning. She'd dressed in a simple white T-shirt and slim jeans paired with bright fuchsia-colored high heels that all seemed effortlessly sexy. Even though nothing should be sexy about a woman who'd kept the secrets she had from him.

And damn, but he couldn't think about what it had

been like to be with her or he'd lose his mind. He'd felt things with her he'd never felt for a woman before, even beyond the electric physical connection. The thought of never being with her again shouldn't twist up his insides like this.

Except, as she withdrew the container of leftover homemade raspberry tarts that she'd shared with him on their flight to Miami just over twenty-four hours ago, he couldn't deny that he still felt drawn to her.

Cursing the attraction, he returned to his email inbox, waiting for a response from Felicia about the status of the samples in the beauty closet. He still didn't have a clear picture about how the final formula had ended up in his father's hands, and he wished he'd hung on to his temper better with Blair to find out more from her.

Only now, with his anger eased and reason returning, he acknowledged how much he'd let his control slip.

Had he really fired a woman who was trying to care for a mother battling cancer? He distinctly remembered how worried she'd been about losing her spot in the brownstone, as well, yet he'd threatened that, too.

As the scent of raspberry tarts drifted through the cabin, reminding him of the kindnesses Blair had shown toward both him and her colleagues—not to mention toward her mom and the other cancer patients at the same facility—Lucas knew he'd overreacted. Because now that cool logic was back in charge, he recognized there was no way she would have done something blatantly illegal, not to mention harmful to his mother.

He believed that with one-hundred-percent certainty, because he knew her character too well to suspect her of something so blatantly wrong. Should she have told him about the solicitations from her former employer?

Absolutely.

Did she deserve to lose a job and a place to live for that?

Of course not. He'd lashed out at her unfairly because his feelings for her were deep. Passionate.

The truth of the matter backhanded him with a slap he deserved. He loved Blair Westcott. He hadn't even known it at the time, but what else explained the uncharacteristic heat and scope of his reaction? He'd been hurt, and he'd reacted badly.

No. Deplorably.

If he'd thought his gut sank when he'd believed she'd been disloyal, it was nothing compared to the way shame and regret dropped him like a stone now. Scrubbing a hand over his face at the thought of the way he'd behaved, he almost didn't hear the captain's warning over the cabin speakers that they were about to land.

The descent only added to his sinking sense that the earth was about to swallow him whole for his stupidity. He needed to talk to her. Not only because he should find out what had really happened, so he could work on fixing this mess for his mom. But also so he could apologize. Assure her that she still had a job, since he had zero authority to fire her in the first place. Let alone any say over her spot in the house.

What the hell had he done?

He wanted to launch himself across the plane and talk to her now. Explain how he'd screwed up and wanted another chance. Not to mention more information about his father's attempts to turn her into a company spy.

But he could hear in his head how self-serving that sounded.

While she tucked the tart container back in her bag and straightened her seat, Lucas told himself to work on a plan first. He couldn't afford to pour more gas on the flames he'd already let fan out of control. He'd have to figure out the right approach. Mull over his options before he said something he'd regret—the way he already had.

For now, he turned his attention back to the laptop and with some difficulty, he was able to focus on his email inbox.

A note from the head of human resources had been sent to his mother, although he'd been cc'd on it.

That seemed strange. Lucas didn't normally get involved in HR matters. Still, remembering his hasty words to Blair, he experienced a knife twist of fear that she'd already turned in a resignation or something like that.

When he clicked on the message, however, it wasn't about Blair.

You should know that Felicia Bell turned in her notice, effectively immediately. Her departure was unorthodox, and she has not completed the exit interview, let alone the other necessary paperwork.

The email continued, but Lucas didn't read beyond that. His gaze returned to the name. Felicia Bell had quit.

The marketing director.

Could it be a coincidence that the same woman who'd tried to implicate Blair had left the company? Could she have been trying to deflect attention from her own activities?

And in an instant, all the things he knew about the leak in Deschamps Cosmetics fell into place, with Felicia at the center.

She hadn't gone to the beauty convention in Miami even though it was the biggest marketing initiative of the year for the company. He'd thought that was peculiar at the time, but Felicia often got a free pass on things because she was a friend of his mom's.

He did a mental head smack as he closed his laptop for landing, knowing he needed to say something to Blair before she walked off this plane and—he feared—out of his life forever.

Not caring about the descent, he rose from his seat to take one across the aisle from her. He couldn't put this off any longer.

"Blair, we need to talk."

His heart hammered when she peered over at him coolly.

"I think we've done more than enough talking for one night."

He hated that he'd hurt her.

And God, he hated the distance he'd put between them. He settled on speaking about a more practical issue.

"Do you think Felicia Bell has a key to the beauty closet?" He needed to confront his father about this. He would take legal action against him. Criminal and civil.

There wasn't a chance he'd allow his mother to be hurt anymore. For that matter, after the way Lucas had treated Blair tonight, he needed to prove to himself that he could be a better man than his father.

He sure hadn't shown it tonight when he'd acted out of self-interest instead of thinking of Blair. He should have relied on what he knew about her instead of the fear he'd felt that she'd betrayed him.

"She's the marketing director," Blair answered automatically, not even bothering to look at him as the lights of Manhattan filled the window to her right. "Of course, she has a key."

Lucas shut his eyes, letting the full weight of his failures fall on his shoulders.

"She's the one who stole the sample."

"Are you sure?" Blair asked, turning wary eyes toward him at last. "Because earlier tonight, you blamed me for the same thing, and you were wrong. The next person you falsely accuse might not take it as well as I have."

"I'm sorry. More sorry than you know." When she didn't respond to his apology he plowed ahead, needing to at least clear up the point about her job. Her home. "Please rest assured that your job is secure at Deschamps. As is your spot in the brownstone. I have no authority over either of them, and I spoke out of turn."

The quiet stretched for so long he wasn't sure she would reply. But as the plane touched down, she finally gave him a level look.

"Thank you for saying I could stay. But I will be turning in my resignation tomorrow—"

"Blair, *please* reconsider."

"If I may finish?" The look she gave him—cool and determined—was so different from the warm, giving woman he knew that the shame and regret only piled higher on his back.

He nodded, recognizing how much he'd screwed up.

"I will turn in my resignation this week, but I will need more time to figure out where to live. I'll discuss it with your mother, however, when I explain to her my conduct in full." She unfastened her seat belt, as the plane slowly taxied on the Teterboro Airport runway. "I have no doubt she will at least hear me out."

Defeat took the air right out of him.

"She will," he agreed, recognizing how much better his mother would handle this than he had. "But I hope you'll give me a chance to explain."

The plane jolted to a halt in the silence. Through the window, he could see the ground crew approach the aircraft.

"Like you gave me a chance?" She shook her head sadly, hitching her bag on one shoulder as she stood. "My mother's illness has taught me that life is too short to spend it with people who don't believe in me. I've shown you the kind of person I am, Lucas. I feel badly I didn't come to you sooner about the request for information on Deschamps, but you could have at least listened to me."

And, without another word, Blair walked to the exit and down the metal stairs. Out of sight. But, God, so very much still in his thoughts. He wasn't surprised when she didn't look back, and she didn't wait to share a vehicle back to the city.

He was surprised how devastated he felt, however. Like his whole world had ended.

Twelve

"Okay, Blair. We have an hour to talk before we're back in Brooklyn," Tana announced from the driver's seat of the rented compact car they'd taken to the Catskills earlier that day.

Sable and Tana had insisted they needed a group outing when Blair had tried to take the train by herself to see her mother that morning. She'd been too heartbroken about Lucas to argue with her friends, letting them rent the car, pick the route and pack a picnic lunch so they could have some fun as well as support Blair during the visit. Only now, on their way home, did she realize how much she'd needed this girl time to keep herself together today.

"Spill. What happened on your trip to Miami? You've dodged talking about it all week."

Blair stared out the window at the traffic on the Palisades Parkway for a moment longer, not sure how to begin to explain the fallout with Lucas. If she talked about it, she was afraid she'd start crying and never stop.

It hurt so much. Because while she might have told Lucas that life was too short to spend it being mistrusted—and she believed that—the aftermath of that declaration was a sleepless night of tears. She'd wanted to see her mother to soak up the comfort of being around someone who loved her uncondition-ally. And maybe that's why she'd let Tana and Sable railroad her into the group trip. She'd known her friends would try to help.

"I've been waiting for this question," she admit-ted, knowing her friends had shown great restraint when she'd called in sick to work for a few days this week before finally submitting her resignation two days ago. "I had the feeling when you were both seized with a need for a road trip that there was more to it than wanting my chicken-salad sandwiches."

"I have no regrets about coercing you into the trip," Sable acknowledged, her elbow sliding be-tween their seats from the back. Always fashion-able, she wore a vintage tracksuit and tennis shoes, accessorized with a bandana to tie back her long hair.

"Although you make the best chicken salad. As in, you could start a restaurant chain with that recipe."

"I've seriously needed a day out of the city, Blair. That much was true." Tana's voice was uncommonly grave, making Blair wonder what was wrong. But before she could ask, Tana continued. "I got some great video footage of a deer behind your mom's cabin. And the shots I took of you doing her makeup turned out really well."

Blair's eyes stung for the hundredth time that day, but for once, not about Lucas. She would treasure the video clips of her friends with her mother. It had been a great visit, and her mom seemed to enjoy the normalcy of meeting some of Blair's friends. She'd forgotten how much her mom enjoyed being around youthful energy.

"Thank you for that." She fished a tissue out of her handbag and wiped her eyes. "I'm glad you came."

"Us, too," Sable declared as Tana swerved to avoid a pothole, pitching them all sideways a little. "Now, what happened in Miami? We saw the photos online of you with Lucas at the conference, and we both agreed you looked ready to have his babies."

Blair couldn't help but let out a watery laugh.

"Maybe I was. But that was before things imploded." Unable to hold it in any longer, she spent the next twenty minutes sharing everything. She started with her own anxiety about hearing from About Face, their repeated job offer to spy on Deschamps Cosmetics for a hefty paycheck, her refusal, the freelance gig she'd accepted and the way she'd been unclear about the nondisclosure agreement. Then she'd laid out what had happened with Lucas, skipping the juicier moments, but being honest about falling for him.

Until he'd broken her heart with his unfounded accusations and willingness to believe the worst about her.

"Oh, honey." Sable rubbed her shoulder as she finished the story. "I'm so sorry. No wonder you're so torn up."

Tana swore softly, slowing the car as they reached the backed-up traffic to cross the George Washington Bridge. "I *warned* him not to hurt you. You're going through too much to deal with this, too."

"What will you do?" Sable passed her a packet of tissues, making Blair realize she'd worn out the one she'd been using.

After tugging one free, she flipped down the mirror on the rental car's sun visor so she could repair her mascara.

"I'm not sure. But I can't work at Deschamps anymore, obviously. I submitted my resignation to HR this week and cc'd Cybil on it." She hadn't opened her email since then, not sure she was ready to see their response to it, or to even know if they'd responded at all.

"Cybil will be disappointed. She seemed so enthusiastic about what a good fit you were there." Sable reached over the back seat into the hatchback and returned with a tablet, which she powered on. "But you're incredibly talented, Blair, and any company would be lucky to scoop you up. Have you thought about what to do next?"

The ever-present anxiety about paying her mother's health-care bills flared up. Had she really just quit her job when she needed that income desperately? How had she let her emotions get the better of her that way?

"That's the problem. I was struggling to afford Mom's care even with the job at Deschamps. I might find something comparable, but I'll still be coming up short every month." She wouldn't even be able to pay the rent on the cabin at this rate.

"You need to think big," Tana mused, silver rings glinting on the steering wheel as she merged in front of a tractor-trailer as easily as if she drove in city traffic every day.

Her friend had an oddly disparate assortment of talents.

"What do you mean?" Blair asked, appreciative of the good driving that she wasn't sure she could have handled as smoothly, despite growing up on Long Island. Manhattan traffic was in a class by itself.

"You need something more than a regular job." Tana glanced over at her from the driver's seat, her dark eyes serious. "You need serious earning potential, and you need it quickly."

"Okay. But what?" She felt incapable of planning for her future when the present was sucking the very life out of her.

She'd been struggling enough to bolster her mom through the treatments, so Blair didn't have the emotional resources to combat the hurt of losing Lucas, too. The toll of those things didn't exactly inspire creative genius to give a new job hunt.

"A low overhead start-up," Sable suggested from the back seat. "Something where you can be your own boss."

The suggestion touched off a spark in her, even though it hardly seemed feasible.

"A high percentage of new businesses fail in the first year," she reminded them, recalling that much from her college courses. She might have had to quit her degree program early to focus on her mom, but she'd paid enthusiastic attention to the entrepreneurial classes. "For that matter, it can take years to start earning a living that way, even if your stay afloat through the first twelve months."

"If you have the right idea at the right time, it doesn't have to take that long." Sable passed her tablet to the front seat. "Scroll through some of those. Plenty of companies have demonstrated big earning power even before venture capitalists come on board."

"Those are anomalies." Blair glanced over the

names, some of them famous, some of them completely unfamiliar.

"Those are risk takers with good ideas." Tana got into the lane to cross the Alexander Hamilton Bridge, making Blair realize the time had flown on the trip home. "And you already have the good idea."

The tablet dropped into her lap as Blair glanced up, startled. "What are you talking about?"

"Providing beauty services to ill or struggling men and women," Sable answered, her lightly perfumed arm reaching between the seats to take back the tablet. "You wanted to start a charitable nonprofit for cancer patients and then expand."

Floored that they remembered, she shook her head. "I don't know that I'm ready to start something like that."

Sable clapped a hand on her shoulder. "Of course you are. All you need is a business plan. Why let your idea languish, when it could make a real difference for people who are hungry to feel normal again?"

Tana cleared her throat before speaking. "Today, when I was filming you, you said that anyone could do makeup on a young, beautiful face. That it was an art when makeup transformed someone's struggle and pain into beauty."

Touched that her friend recalled the words so readily, she was speechless.

Sable, however, had more to say. She shifted so that she spoke to Tana. "We could use that clip to pitch the idea, couldn't we? You and I could go through the footage tonight. Show Blair in action, and use her own words like a voiceover."

"For what purpose?" Blair asked, mind struggling to keep up when her heart was so heavy.

The day before at this same time, she and Lucas were leaving the Miami Convention Center, rushing to their suite to follow their attraction to its natural, red-hot conclusion.

What a difference a day made.

"That's actually not a bad idea." Tana's thumbs rapped out a soft rhythm on the steering wheel, her silver rings clinking gently. "I've been wanting to do more postproduction work. It's not like I'm getting many auditions lately, anyhow."

"We could crowdfund it—" Sable said, then Blair interrupted.

"Guys. I'll be okay. You don't need to do all this." She was overwhelmed at their generosity. Their willingness to come to her rescue. "I couldn't accept that kind of help, and it's not like I could apply start-up funds for a charitable non-profit toward my mother's health care."

Tana headed south through the Bronx, the traffic easing slightly. "We could separate them out. Use a different platform for the hospital bills, but link to it from the business crowdfund."

Sable snapped her fingers. "That's perfect."

"No." Blair shook her head, needing to head this

off before they invested any more time in solving problems that she needed to fix. "I can't let you do all this for Mom and me."

"I'm not sure you can stop the efforts of well-meaning friends, Blair." Tana shrugged a careless shoulder like it wasn't a big deal. "We want to help. And you could use some assistance right now."

She released a breath, shaken at how worn out she felt. She did feel like she'd been shouldering a lot for the last year. "It's all so sudden. I'm not really prepared to start a new business right now."

"But you're passionate about it, which means you will do a great job on it," Sable assured her, taking a sip from her bottle of water before tucking it in the cup holder. "You should at least consider it. For your mom's sake, if not for yourself."

The words expressed what mattered most to Blair. And even before the car pulled up to their door at the brownstone, she knew she would go along with the plan. The business idea had been hers to start with anyhow, she'd just shoved it to the back burner, thinking it wasn't the right time for it. But what if it was?

She did need help now, and she felt fortunate that her friends had her back when she needed them most.

It just still hurt to think she'd confided some of the same things to Lucas that she'd told her friends. And while they turned her words into a business opportunity, he had only keyed in to her admission that she'd spoken to her former employer, turning that into a confession of disloyalty.

She really needed to lavish her love and attention on friends who deserved it, instead of a man who clearly did not.

Except it still wasn't that clear to her heart.

No matter how often she told herself to forget about Lucas, she knew there wasn't any chance of making that happen.

After the ill-fated trip to Miami, Lucas spent most of the week racking up attorney fees to address the stolen-formula crisis with his father.

He'd needed consultation and outside legal expertise specializing in corporate law and intellectual property rights. He'd spent hours tracking down Deschamps Cosmetics' various security policies, confidentiality agreements in house and their formal document-control procedures. In addition, he'd thoroughly researched industrial-espionage regulations for himself, and then carefully reviewed the best way to file federal charges.

He hadn't even started looking into filing a civil suit. For the moment, he just hoped he had enough to convince his father he was serious about going after him.

Taking a break from his work, he stood from his temporary office in the Deschamps Cosmetics midtown headquarters and walked to the window overlooking the Hudson and—in the distance—the Statue of Liberty.

The view was one of the best Manhattan had to offer.

Yet he didn't really see it. He found himself remembering a different waterfront view. A stormy Atlantic Ocean with Blair at his side, while raindrops from a summer shower glistened on her cheek.

He couldn't stop thinking about her. Not even burying himself in boring reading about security policies could ease vivid memories of the hurt he'd put in her eyes. Or the cool way she'd walked away from him, reminding him that time was too precious to waste on people who didn't believe in her.

The words had circled in his head ever since. Louder sometimes. Softer others. But always there.

When his phone rang, he couldn't help a spike of hope that it would be her. Which, of course, it was not.

"Hello, Mom," he answered a moment later, leaning a shoulder into the window high above the West Side Highway. "I'm still working on the response to Dad, but we've got a solid case."

It blew his mind that it might come to this—taking legal action against his own father. Was it any surprise that trust didn't come easily to Lucas when he couldn't trust his own dad? He'd thought he'd dealt with his anger toward his father, but he resented that the issue had spilled over to taint what Lucas had with Blair all too briefly.

But now, he needed to reassure his mother. They'd only spoken about business since the night she'd called him in Miami with the news that had imploded his relationship with Blair, but he'd tried to keep her updated on his progress with filing charges against his father. Most of their conversations had concerned the news that Felicia, his mother's one-time friend, had stolen the sample to pass onto Peter Deschamps. His mom hadn't been as shocked as he'd anticipated. Apparently Felicia had always hoped to catch Peter's eye, and figured she finally had a way of drawing attention to herself. For his part, Lucas had already filed formal charges against the Deschamps Cosmetics former marketing director.

"Hello to you, too, and I'm sure you'll figure something out, darling," his mother said absently, her voice calm. Thoughtful, even. A far cry from how rattled she'd been when she'd first phoned him in Miami. "I have a question for you about something else."

"I'll try to answer if I can." He glanced back at his desk and the two chairs across from it, remembering when he'd asked Blair up to his office to talk to her about finding the leak in the organization.

He'd taken the wrong approach with her from the very beginning. But that didn't diminish how much he'd enjoyed getting to know her. Growing to care about her.

Love her.

"I told you that I received Blair's resignation." She'd texted him about that the day prior, sending him a copy of the letter.

Lucas hadn't had the heart to open it.

"I remember," he said shortly, not ready to talk about what had happened between them. Maybe a part of him still hoped he'd be able to fix it somehow.

Or maybe he simply didn't want to admit how he'd leaped to conclusions that had wounded her deeply.

"But have you been following her new business venture online?"

Lucas pulled his thoughts from the old memories and tried to dial into what his mother had just told him.

"I'm sorry. What was that?" He straightened from his slouch against the window, giving the call his full attention.

"Blair has launched a crowdfunding initiative for a new business to bring beauty services to ill women and men, starting with cancer patients. She's also mentioned the possibility of a future clean makeup line that's safe, non-toxic, and comes with transparent labeling of ingredients," his mother explained, relating news that he hadn't heard, even if the business idea was very familiar to him.

Good for her.

"She mentioned to me that she wanted to do something like that." He couldn't keep the pride in Blair from his voice, though he wished he'd done more to help her achieve her dream. He'd lost the chance to be at her side now, and he was still furious with himself about that.

How had he let his mistrust blind him?

"Yes. Well, I wish she'd come to me with the idea. This is exactly the kind of initiative I would love to be a part of." His mother sounded disappointed, but if he wasn't mistaken, a bit proud of Blair, too. "Did you know her mother is battling ovarian cancer right now?"

"Yes. I'm aware." He closed his eyes, wishing he'd done more. Wishing he hadn't been idiot enough to threaten her job at the worst possible time in her life. "Where are you learning about all this, by the way?"

"It's all over social media," she explained. "Haven't you been online today? The video that accompanies the business pitch is just…well, it's breathtaking, Lucas. There's a video credit to Tana Blackstone, my other brownstone resident. I chose such talented young women as tenants."

This time, the pride in his mom's voice was unmistakable.

Charging toward his desk, he fired up the laptop and searched Blair's name. The photo results that populated the screen included the image of them together at the beauty conference, a picture that still sucker punched him with how right they looked to-gether.

How in love, damn it.

But next to that picture, there was a still from a video, and it showed Blair sweeping a makeup brush along the cheekbone of a woman whose features mirrored Blair's own in thirty more years. The woman had a pink scarf tied around her head, a silver hummingbird pin clipped at an angle in the center. The tenderness in Blair's eyes made his throat tighten.

Lucas had to swallow hard before he spoke again. "I'm going to check this out now, Mom. Was there anything else?"

His mother made a soft, scoffing sound. "Yes, son. Of course, there's something else. I want you to fix whatever happened between you and Blair to make her resign. Swallow your pride, ask her to come back, tell her I want to sponsor everything she's doing. Just…make it right."

Propping an elbow on the desk, he allowed his forehead to fall onto his hand and closed his eyes. The weight of what he'd done made his shoulders slump, and he found the truth pouring from him.

"I really messed up, Mom. I don't know if she'll take me back."

Trust was a fragile thing. And he'd stomped all over it. This relationship business was so far out of his wheelhouse it was laughable.

"Sometimes half the battle is recognizing you

were in the wrong," his mother advised with a sigh, before her tone turned speculative. "Although…does she know you love her?"

He lifted his head. "How do *you* know I love her?"

She made a tsking sound. "Oh, Lucas. One look at the photo of you two together told me that. But *I'm* your mother. She's a talented young woman, but she probably doesn't have my same skill in reading you."

"You think I should tell her that, even though she's already told me I don't have a shot with her anymore?" His gaze scanned the article that went with the video. He already knew his mother was right.

"Absolutely, you have to tell her. Love changes everything, Lucas. Just because my marriage didn't work out doesn't mean that love isn't worth fighting for."

Her wise words settled on him with a total rightness, and a reluctant smile curved his lips at his mother's insight. He'd never told her that he avoided relationships because of the collateral damage from his parents' marriage. But maybe he hadn't needed to.

"I'm not sure how you know so much, but I think you're right."

"I may be a fierce and successful businesswoman, but the accomplishment I am most proud of in my life is being a good mother." She drew in a deep breath. "If your dad manages to buy Deschamps Cosmetics, it's not going to ruin me, because I have something far more important that he's never learned to value."

"We're going to keep the company, Mom." He'd paid enough in attorney fees to be reasonably sure of that. "I'll fight this to the end."

"Thank you, my son, and I do mean that. But I have what matters most in my life. Do you know what your father never learned to value?"

Lucas smiled at his mom's tenacity in making her point. "What's that?"

"Love, darling. Haven't you been listening? It's the only thing that matters. Now, go win back our girl."

Thirteen

"Do you like the Linzer cookies more or the thumbprints?" Blair asked her roommates while music blasted in their kitchen. "This is a serious question to help me decide which cookies I'm going to send my biggest donors as a thank-you."

She'd been baking for hours, with trays full of treats to show for it and no peace of mind like she normally found at the oven. She'd invited Sable and Tana to be her taste testers since she needed the treats to be perfect and she didn't trust her concentration these days.

But still she baked.

And baked.

She didn't know how else to keep her thoughts on the success of their crowdfunding venture instead of thinking about Lucas, and how she'd probably never see him again. Or if she did, it would only be to escort her from the brownstone when Cybil kicked her out of the house. It hurt to think about him, and all Blair had lost.

"You're not really serious about that?" Tana asked from her perch on a counter stool, her brown hair dyed lilac at the tips to match her new purple leather pants that she liked so much she claimed she wasn't taking them off for a month. "Blair, you'll be the first entrepreneur in history who rewards investors with homemade cookies."

"Who says it's a reward? Maybe it's a bribe so they'll invest even more." She couldn't believe how quickly the idea had taken off, mostly thanks to the expert pitch video her friends had made. She was glad for her mother's sake, and still the victory felt hollow without someone special by her side. "Although I guess I shouldn't be greedy. I'm already floored by how much you've raised."

Her amazing friends had made a video that explained her idea for delivering beauty services into the home as a way to nurture the spirit for people suffering health problems. The video had been viewed an extraordinary number of times, with people from all over the world praising the idea, contributing to the start-up, and sharing personal cancer-survivor stories.

That alone had overwhelmed her, as the fund had quickly accumulated more than enough money to allow her to begin providing services. But then, there was a link on that pitch page for people who wanted to contribute to Amber Westcott's medical bills. The link had a short video of its own, which featured her mother showing the cabin in the foothills of the Catskills. There was also a snippet of Mom's friend Valerie talking about how brave her friend had been through her treatments, and even photos from her mother's life back in Long Island, where she'd coached girls field hockey and waited tables in a popular restaurant. Blair hadn't even realized how much Tana had filmed during their visit, especially of the small photo album her mom kept on the coffee table.

She'd sobbed buckets when she watched the piece, especially when her mom had talked about how much of a help Blair had been to her throughout her cancer journey. Hearing that—words her mom hadn't ever said directly to her—had healed a little wound in her that she hadn't realized lingered. But the bottom line was the community outpouring of support and generosity had been epic. Blair wouldn't have to worry about bills for a while.

She just wished she could share some of her excitement about that good fortune with Lucas. Which made no sense given the way he'd treated her.

"How much *you've* raised," Sable corrected her, pointing at her with a snowball cookie, a bit of flaked coconut falling to the plate. Today's outfit was a flame-red sheathe dress that hugged her small baby bump. "The idea is all yours. And these snowballs are underrated. I think they could be a contender for winning best thank-you cookie."

"The production crew deserves most of the thank-you cookies, though," Tana clarified as she reached for samples off two other cooling racks. "And as head producer, my money is on these gingersnaps."

The doorbell chimed then, the resonant sound vibrating a small speaker over the stairway.

"Are we expecting anyone?" Sable asked, hopping off her counter stool to walk into the vacant front bedroom on the garden floor where, Blair knew, Sable would peer out the window at street level to see if she recognized the visitor's feet.

She returned a moment later, her hazel eyes opened wide. "It's Lucas."

Blair took a step back at the news. Her friends stared at her, no doubt waiting for her reaction.

Her belly flipped, senses humming at the prospect of being close to him. But she was also plenty wary at the thought of more heartache.

"Do you *want* to see him?" Tana asked, studying her carefully. "Or do you want me to send him packing?"

"I'm not sure," Blair whispered, jumping at the timer going off on the oven.

She withdrew a cookie sheet filled with almond tassies. She was nervous but very curious to know what he wanted.

"We can screen him for you." Sable hooked her thumb toward the stairs. "Tana and I will go ask him a few questions and you can hear what he has to say from down here. If you like how it's going, come up. If you don't—"

"Then we'll toss him on his ear," Tana said, finishing for her, her combat boots already thunking their way up the steps. "I know a self-defense move that might work on him."

Blair's stomach clenched.

She knew he'd spoken to her unfairly, but did she want to hold one night against him when he'd been upset on his mother's behalf? She understood how much he wanted to save the business for Cybil's sake. Hearing his mother rattled and shaken over the phone that evening would have been tough on him. He hadn't been able to hear Blair out when he'd been in the middle of a crisis.

It wasn't a good reason, but it was a reason. Did Blair have any justification for not listening to Lucas now? Especially when she'd had evidence that might have helped him in his search for the real leak in the company?

Clearing a spot on the counter for the hot tray, Blair set it on a trivet, then shut off the oven before moving to the foot of the stairs to listen.

As security details went, Blair couldn't have chosen a more intimidating pair. At least, not as far as Lucas was concerned.

Her roommates stood on the threshold of the building, their folded-arm stances mirroring one another while they took his measure.

Seventies rock music spilled out the door from behind them. The taller brunette wore a red dress and heels, eyes broadcasting a don't-mess-with-me vibe while she frowned at him. The petite fury in purple pants next to her looked ready to rumble in her spiked bracelets and boots, her expression downgraded to outright scowl. If these women wanted his blood, he had zero defense against them.

"Hello." He plastered on what he hoped was a pleasant expression. "Is Blair home?"

"Why? So you can fire her again?" Tana, the shorter one, asked, taking a half step forward.

Just enough to almost crowd him but not quite.

This reception didn't bode well. But even if it was no less than he deserved, he needed this chance to talk to Blair.

"That was a mistake. I already made it clear

to Blair that I misspoke. My mother is extremely grieved to lose her." He peered past the two women into the darkened parlor floor, but he saw no sign of Blair.

The music came from downstairs. The scents of almond, sugar and vanilla wafted up, scents that normally clung to the woman he loved.

Blair was down there. His *world* was down there.

"What would you say to Blair if we let you see her?" Sable asked, flipping her long dark hair behind one shoulder.

And, perhaps, shifting subtly so that his voice would carry past her to wherever Blair listened?

It was just a hunch, but he felt in his blood that she was close by. Beyond the delicious smell of her baking, he could sense her nearness in the defensiveness of the friends who'd bolstered Blair when he'd failed her so miserably.

He owed these women a debt for that. But right now, his number-one concern was saying the right thing to win an audience with the person who held his heart.

"Before anything else, I'd start by telling her how proud I am of her for having enough faith in her idea—and in herself—to start her own business. It takes a lot of courage to do that, and I know she will make it a success." He glanced from Tana to Sable and back again. "I know you two had a lot to do with that. The video showcased Blair's compassion really well."

He'd teared up watching the exchange between mother and daughter as Blair lovingly shadowed her mom's eyes, talking about bringing out the sparkle that she remembered from her childhood. The piece was emotional, yes. But it also got across the way a few moments of pampering could make an ill person feel more normal.

A moment later, Lucas saw a shadow on the stairs from the kitchen just before a blond head came into view. Relief poured through him, followed by an urgent need to pull her into his arms. Except he didn't have that right.

He needed to focus on her first, or he might never have the right again. The possibility reminded him how much was riding on this conversation.

"I'll talk to him," Blair announced, her eyes on him as she wiped her hands on a white apron with a ruffled edge of fabric printed with bright red cherries.

When she turned to one side, he could see she wore a pair of frayed jean shorts beneath the apron, along with a pink tank top. Her hair was in a ponytail, her face free of makeup. A little flour still smudged one cheek.

As she edged between her friends to where he stood, Sable smoothed a thumb across the flour spot to remove it. Then, her friends disappeared back down the stairs.

Leaving him alone with Blair in the doorway.

"Would you like to sit out on the roof?" she asked, untying the apron and slipping it off. "It's nice enough outside."

Memories of the last time he'd spent with her there gripped him by the throat. Did she still remember that time with fondness? Or was she only inviting him up there to replace that memory with her final good riddance? Tension tightened his shoulders.

"I'd like that. Thank you."

A moment later, he followed her up three flights to the heavy steel door that led to the rooftop patio.

"Have a seat." She gestured to the furniture, but instead of settling on the outdoor couch like the last time, she dropped into an armchair diagonally situated from the small cushioned sofa.

The summer evening was still young as sounds from the street drifted up to them—car engines, church bells tolling the hour, live music that might be coming from the park. But the dwarf trees around the roof's perimeter dulled the noise a bit, making their retreat feel private.

He turned toward her, knowing this was a make-or-break moment. Everything rode on how well he laid out his case.

"Thank you for seeing me, Blair. I know you weren't interested in my apology that night on the plane, but I deeply regret not listening to you when you tried to tell me what happened." He started there, feeling like he'd done an inadequate job with apologizing before and knowing she deserved the words.

"It was a night of high stress and emotion," she conceded, tucking a finger under her tattered friendship bracelet and smoothing it flat. "We probably both could have done a better job of listening."

Surprised that she'd offered this glimpse of empathy, he felt the first nudge of, if not hope, at least the possibility for a better outcome. For forgiveness, perhaps.

"I deserved the way you shut me down, Blair. I had no business accusing you of something so—" He still couldn't believe how he'd let himself think she'd steal from him. From his mother. "Something you would never have done. There is no excuse for it, but maybe it would help a little to know that trust comes hard for me after the way I was raised."

Damn it, he didn't want to sound like some kind of whiny rich kid who had life so hard, because that was patently untrue. She didn't speak, waiting for him to finish.

"All I mean to say is this. I couldn't trust my own father, who has always been a liar and a cheat." And yet that didn't fully explain it, either. Why had he been so quick to jump down her throat at the news the formula had been passed to his father?

He drew in a deep breath, bracing himself for the

rest of what he wanted—needed—to say to her. Win or lose, he had to give his all. "It made me wary. Before I met you, Blair, I was determined to spend my life on my own to avoid the kind of heartache my dad put Mom through."

Blair tried to pick through what he was saying, her heart hammering wildly at his words and to be near him after days apart.

Had it really been just a couple of weeks ago that she'd been sharing his bed, falling head over heels for him? So much had happened in a short space of time. She studied him in his short-sleeved gray silk polo shirt and dark pants. He was a sight for her lonely eyes, even though everything between them was different now.

Plus, she had a business to grow, but at least her financial worries were eased. If only she could get her mother through this disease. And, heaven help her, if only she could rewind to the way things had been between her and Lucas.

"Before you met me," she said, mentally repeating what he'd just told her. "Does that mean, after you met me, you were considering...*not* spending your life alone?"

A promising idea. The possibility made her sit up straighter in her seat. At first, she'd wondered if Cybil had twisted Lucas's arm into coming over here to apologize. She knew that her former boss was disappointed about her resignation. And from a few things in the letter Cybil had emailed her the day after Blair quit, she'd guessed that Cybil had been hopeful Lucas and Blair would reconcile.

But maybe Lucas wasn't here just because his mother had wanted to smooth things over.

Maybe he cared more about her than he'd let on.

Lucas shifted to the edge of the couch that put him closest to her chair. So close his knee brushed her bare one.

"Blair, meeting you turned my whole world on its ear—in a good way—right up until that last night together. You baffled me from the first time I saw you, passing out cookies around the office like some kind of crazy sexy den mother in your pink dresses and sweet manners."

"Den mother?" She wrinkled her nose, not following.

Although she liked the *crazy sexy* bit.

"I've never met anyone like you," he explained, his voice low but intense. "You seemed so good, so sweet, I didn't think you could be real. I decided before I even got to know you that you had to be the spy."

Stunned, she frowned at him, wondering what that possibly meant. "You took me to Miami thinking I was stealing company secrets?"

"No. Definitely not. By the time we had that kiss, right here on this rooftop—the same night I learned that you took care of a sick mother—I knew that you really were as good and sweet as you seemed." He spread his arms wide, hands splayed to show his confusion. "I'm just trying to explain how I've been a step behind you this whole time, never quite making sense of how you could be so damned amazing."

"I'm not good or amazing. I bake to relieve stress and because it reminds me of happy times with my mother. It's not because I want to be the office good fairy." She folded her arms around herself, not sure why his picture of her rankled so much, but she wanted this man's love, not his admiration, as though she was some sort of glorified Girl Scout. "And I irritate my own mother so much she has to shove me out the door at the end of our visits because I hover."

"I'm not expressing myself well." Lucas reached out to lay his hand on her knee, his touch conveying things his words hadn't.

She'd missed his touch.

Missed *him*.

"So try harder," she whispered, willing him to feel about her even a fraction of the way she felt about him. "What did you really come here for?"

His tawny eyes flashed with emotion. Heat. "I came to tell you that I love you."

"You…what?" She did a double take, needing him to repeat that part.

Her pulse raced. She held her breath, tuning her

ears to the frequency of his voice so she didn't miss a syllable.

"I love you, Blair. I know that I wronged you and that I'm not expressing myself well, and that I've been a step behind this whole time—"

"Oh, Lucas." One moment she was in her chair, the next she was in his arms and on his lap. Sprawling over him. Squeezing him. "I love you, too."

Unlike her, he didn't need her to say it twice.

His strong arms wound tight around her, holding her like he'd never let go. She closed her eyes, tipping her forehead to his shoulder, soaking up the feel of his warmth.

His love.

The joy of it felt like a flower blooming inside her, filling her up with a hope and promise of so many more happy times to come.

"The last few days have been pure hell," he confided against the top of her head between kisses to her hair. Then, he edged back to look at her, still cradling her against him. "I wanted to come here so many times, but I kept remembering how you walked away. I was afraid you'd never listen to me again."

"I felt so broken that night on the flight home. I needed to leave before I fell apart in front of you." She'd never forget the way her legs had felt like wood as she'd left him on the tarmac.

"I'll never doubt you again, Blair. I stand by what I said. You're too good for me to mistrust you."

She shook her head, knowing that life didn't work that way. Not even love worked that way.

"You're entitled to have doubts. I'm sure I'll have moments of doubt, too. But next time, we'll talk it through." She stroked a hand over his face, feeling the bristle against her jaw and wanting to kiss him there. "We'll assume the best about each other before we let the doubts take over."

His tawny eyes tracked hers while his hands roamed over her thigh and back, feeling her body as if he couldn't get enough of her. She felt exactly that same way.

"I'm new to this, Blair, but I promise I'm going to do everything in my power to make you happy. All the time." The sincerity was unmistakable, and it made her toes curl inside her tennis shoes.

"I believe you." She couldn't wait to feel the depth of that sincerity when they were in her bed together.

She planned to keep him there all night long. Maybe for days on end.

"You always have a job at Deschamps, by the way." He kissed his way down her neck, giving her shivers. "My mother was adamant that I win you back."

"She was?"

"Apparently she could tell I was in love with you after seeing the photos of us together in Miami."

Blair edged back, a hint of worry returning.

"What about her company? Is she going to have to sell to your dad?"

"Not a chance. I've already emailed the board members about Dad's coercion and threats. They know I'm prepared to press charges and make this public if he doesn't back off." He stroked her hair, his touch easing her as much as his words. "Even if he isn't personally deterred, his board can and will rein him in."

Around them, the leaves on the dwarf trees rustled. A wind chime on the next rooftop over sounded a few random notes.

"Good." She took a deep breath. It felt like the first time she'd been able to breathe for days. No, months. The worries about her mother's health care had weighed her down far more than she realized, and thanks to her friends, at least the financial anxiety had been eased. "Now I just need to get my mom well and all will be right with my world."

His expression turned solemn. He tipped her face toward him so they could look at one another squarely.

"I know I can't promise you that she will get better, but you realize I'll do everything in my power to help ensure she gets everything she needs?"

Her chest warmed inside at that assurance, warmth bathing the backs of her eyes.

"Thank you, Lucas."

"I love you, Blair." He kissed one eye and then the other. "I can't wait to show you how much."

She wound her arms around his neck, the import of his words making her heart feel too full. She couldn't hold so much happiness inside.

"I'm free for a couple of hours until I need to start packaging up the baked goods for delivery." She skimmed her hands along his shoulders, savoring the feel of his warmth and strength. "We could go downstairs, and you could get a start on trying to show me."

He rose to his feet so fast, with her in his arms, that her head spun. She whooped out loud, laughing, as he carried her away to start their future together.

* * * * *

If you love
Blair and Lucas,
you won't want to miss
Tana's story,
The Stakes of Faking It,
by USA TODAY *bestselling author*
Joanne Rock.
Coming November 2021
from Harlequin Desire.